ARENA PLANET

118 Providence

ARENA PLANET

By

Mike Lynch & Brandon Barr

SILVER LEAF BOOKS

HOLLISTON, MASSACHUSETTS

ARENA PLANET

Copyright © 2016 by Mike Lynch & Brandon Barr

Cover Art by Shutterstock.

First printing September 2016
10 9 8 7 6 5 4 3 2 1

ISBN # 1-60975-161-2
ISBN-13 # 978-1-60975-161-6
LCCN # 2016946749

Silver Leaf Books, LLC
P.O. Box 6460
Holliston, MA 01746
+1-888-823-6450

Visit our web site at www.SilverLeafBooks.com

To Chris Fik, whom I once beat in wrestling.

- Brandon

ARENA PLANET

CHAPTER 1

Still unsure if he had covered his tracks, Carter Stone walked down the steps of St. Patrick's Cathedral and looked at his hands. No matter how many times he'd washed them, the blood of the men he'd killed always felt like a stain on his soul. He wiped his fingers against the side of his black jeans.

He was done with the whole thing. Finished. After a lifetime of crime, he no longer had the stomach for it.

Five long months before, he had been given a contract that should have been no different than the others—take out his boss's rival in a staged accident, and then he'd disappear into the woodwork until the heat died down. When he had read in the newspaper the next day it had been the target's daughter driving the car instead of her father, something snapped inside. He hadn't been able to get the girl's smiling face out of his head since. He wanted to get way. Far, far away. A simple place in the mountains he could call his own. That should wash away his pain. Just one problem. His oath that bound him to the cartel.

"Know the truth, and the truth will make you free."

Those words cut deep into Carter's soul. The priest said it to Clarence, the next man he was supposed to kill, as he waited for him in the church portico. Freedom. Was such a thing possible?

As he observed the two talk, Carter mulled over those ten simple words. Not just words, but daggers that cut into him without mercy, revealing the truth he could no longer deny—his life had been a waste.

It was Clarence's confession to the priest of all he he'd done wrong over the years, buttressed by the regret in his voice that finally pushed Carter into the light. He slipped his gun with the silencer back into his pocket and waited. That's when the two came up with their plan.

Carter splattered him with chicken's blood, then snapped three pictures. Convincing enough of the "hit" the two of them thought.

Clarence thanked him with tears in his eyes under the visage of a pale Christ. "Go and sin no more," Clarence quoted. "That's what the man said to that woman at the well. Just like that, she's free. The priest told me so. You know how many good men I turned crooked? I can't even remember. And now I'm free. Just like that."

The words burned in Carter's ears as he walked down the church steps. Burned but did not heal. It was one thing to turn a man bad. It was another to cut him down in the prime of life and toss his lifeless body into the East River, all the while thinking about what he wanted for dinner that night.

He felt it now though.

From his pocket, he fished out his Bluetooth and glanced at the crowded downtown street as he slipped it into his ear, then up at the sky. Hanging like a dark ominous cloud was the massive spacecraft that had been suspended above New York City for the past couple of weeks. It looked like the Millennium Falcon on steroids. Why it had come was anyone's guess.

Carter punched in a number on his phone.

At first, people couldn't talk about anything else after it arrived, both on the streets, and on the news. But then a strange thing happened. After a few days, the novelty had begun to wear off. It was as though an alien ship floated above New York since there was a New York. Now, it felt like another fixture in the city, the same as the Empire State Building or the Statue of Liberty.

"Lenny's pizza," came the nasal voice on the receiver.

"It's Stone. I did it. Clarence is dead."

"Have a change of heart, did you?"

"Clarence was my last hit. I'm done. You can find yourself a new killer."

"...Not so fast," said Lenny. "You have Carmen a little worried. A lot of people find their tongue loosening when they try to leave the family. You know better than anyone about that."

Carter stared out at the passersby on the street. He did know about that. He'd killed nine narcs in the five short years for the family. He'd killed others too for various reasons. Killing was his business. But after what the priest had said to Clarence, he wanted out.

He looked down at his hands. He swore they had a red tint to them, stained, as if the blood of every person he executed had soaked like tattoo ink into his skin.

He clenched his fist, suddenly furious.

"I'm out Lenny! Tell Carmen I'll die with his secrets, even if I have to choke on them."

"That's nice," said Lenny. "Do you know how many of the people you knocked off told him something similar? All of them. And did any of them tell him in person. Not one. Do you see the pattern, Stone? He ain't gonna trust you any more than a pit bull that's been beat with a bat its whole life. Now you come in, and we'll talk."

Carter almost hung up. "You think you can talk me into more killing? Or do you have some kind of job for your ex-hitmen who've suddenly gained a conscience?" He was wasting time. He had to leave the city. "What's the point of coming in? So you can knock me off easy?"

"Shut it, Stone... I'm beginning to wonder if you did the job at all. Is Clarence really dead?"

"Two rounds to the heart."

"Where'd you do it?"

"St. Patrick's Cathedral."

"You killed him in a church?"

"That's right," he lied. "The guy practically lived in there. Never came out. The priests were bringing him food and water."

Carter heard someone shouting on the sidewalk. Across the street, a man pointed up at the sky. Everyone around him stopped and looked up. Carter threw a glance in the same direction, and saw it. Something was coming down from the ship. Some kind of swirling light.

Lenny's nasally voice suddenly burst in his ear, "I'm calling you a liar, Stone. You tell me you have this religious moment a week ago, how you can't kill anymore, and then you go and shoot the guy in church. I don't believe it."

"I have pictures."

"Piss on your pictures, Stone. You don't think I smell something rotten. Where's the body?"

"I threw it in the dumpster. Covered it with some cardboard boxes."

"Alright Stone, I'm sending a guy to the church right now.

Then I'll know you're not a lying sack of manure. If Clarence is in that dumpster, then we can talk."

A scream tore the air.

Carter kept his attention fixed on the conversation. "Lenny, you tell Carmen to forget me, or I swear, if I get wind the family is coming after me, I'll sing so loud the entire city will be humming my tune."

Tires screeched on the street. Carter looked up just in time to see a taxi smash the back of a Porsche. Then he noticed the people. Everyone was running and pointing.

Wind whipped his hair. The swirling light was coming straight for him.

Carter sprinted down the steps and found sidewalk. A sharp screech grabbed his attention. Ahead of the light, a taxicab jumped the curb. People on the sidewalk dove out of its way as it passed them. Carter stopped. A familiar face peered out from the passenger seat and from behind the wheel. He had a gun in his hand and a smile on his face.

All Carter had time to do was jump. He hit the hood and the impact rocked his body like a doll into the window. Glass cracked against his back, and then he was airborne over the back end of the cab. Everything spun around him until his body hit the sidewalk hard.

Dazed, he tried to stand, then crumbled over.

More tires squealed. The effect pulled him out of his state of semi-consciousness. Despite the pain in his arms and back, he managed to pull his head off the concrete and look.

As though in a dream, the cab sped towards him in reverse. Unable to move, he laid down flat and looked up. If this was it, he didn't want to see the car as it hit him at full throttle.

The bright swirling air whipped overhead like a tornado and sucked up every Christmas light in New York.

Carter felt his body lift—consciousness ebbed in and out—the roar of the cab's engine faded into silence.

Then, everything went dark. A numbing wind bit at his bones and he opened his eyes. To his surprise, he found himself staring at the city skyline from above. In the distance, the Statue of Liberty rose out of the New York Harbor. She stared at him with the same placid expression that his boss, Carmen, had whenever he assigned him his next hit.

Carter laughed. He'd been rescued by the damn aliens. He pictured Carmen's face when he heard the news that the spacecraft had whisked him away. His soulless lips curling into a frown.

The image faded, as did the exhilaration over not being a human stain drug over a quarter mile of sidewalk.

As the spacecraft twice the size of Central Park swallowed him, the question of what he would face became a sobering reality.

The pale-faced visage of the Christ he remembered from the church bore into his mind.

He swore.

Whatever was about to happen, he felt sure it was some kind of retribution from above for the body count he'd accumulated.

Perhaps it would have been better to have been a human sidewalk hamburger.

He was about to find out.

CHAPTER 2

The inside of the ship embodied pure darkness. No sounds, only a faint popcorn-tinged scent mixed with a strange other-worldly odor. He felt himself dropped lightly onto something hard. He winced as shooting pain shot down his leg. Probably the left over bite from the taxi hitting him at forty miles-an-hour.

Gingerly, Carter touched his hands against the alien floor. It felt cold and metallic, like an aluminum bat.

He tried to stand, but fell onto his back with a grunt. The pain in his leg was more serious then he first thought. Much more serious. Something was broken.

A low mechanical whine sounded above his head, and a light shot all around him. A shadowy shape floated into the room, large, like a grand piano, but with arm-like things dangling off of it.

It wasn't the type of alien Carter had expected. He'd pictured the big bug-eyed creatures he'd seen in comics as a kid. One particular image had been burned into his memory. A close-up of a bug-eyed green man holding something unpleasantly shaped in his hand. An anal probe, as Carter recalled.

He tightened his butt cheeks. They wouldn't take him with-out a fight.

Suddenly, his hand went for the forty-five mag in his coat pocket. He'd sworn he'd never kill again. But he also felt no qualms against putting a half dozen slugs into something shaped like a Steinway grand.

He removed his hand from the gun. Better to let the alien make the first move.

As the thing hovered closer, he saw the glint of metal. It wasn't an alien, it was some kind of blasted robot.

A whirring noise reverberated from the machine, and a metal tube extended out from the thing like a hose. Carter's eyes narrowed on the tip.

Several sharp clicks went off in quick succession, and a needle popped out like a five inch switchblade. Carter's hand sprang for the gun.

A red glow pierced his eyes. Hot, like fire. When it felt like he couldn't take one more second of this medieval examination, his entire body went rigid. No matter how he tried to move, his muscles no longer responded. The needle dove into his leg. He would have shouted in pain if he could. This place, it seemed, didn't permit physical displays of disapproval.

Another whirring sound vibrated in his ear. Something clamped down hard on his head and then he felt pressure against the top of his skull.

He screamed inside as something bore through his hair and into his cranium. The agony drove deeper, until he wanted to die—and then the drilling stopped and darkness swarmed in. He couldn't see, but it felt like a corkscrew had gone through the top of his skull and popped the top off. Desperate to get away, he found he still couldn't move.

Carter focused on breathing to distract himself from the intense pain igniting his raw synapses, then something cool squirted from the needle that had driven deep into his brain. It spread like water trickling through his body. The ordeal finally relented, and in its place was a warm, soothing fire that he knew must have been some kind of drug. His senses dulled. No longer afraid, he simply drifted away for a time.

Sounds slowly drew him out of his wooziness. He felt like he had downed a liter of hard liquor and had just come out of the stupor. The same amount of liquor he drank the night after he made a kill.

A groan sounded above him.

Carter oriented himself. He laid flat on his back against something hard and cold. Fighting against the warm fire of the drugs tingling under his skin, Carter struggled to sit up.

A man in a camouflaged green and black mesh uniform lay face down on the floor. Carter noticed a Russian flag on his shoulder with strange characters: спецназ.

There was something odd about his head. It looked like a metal cockroach with two legs extended into his ears. Instinctively, Carter reached up and patted his own head where the drilling had been done. His fingers touched cold, plated metal, just like the Russian's.

What were these things?

"America?" said a voice behind him.

Carter spun, his hand darting for the gun in his jacket. It was gone.

An Asian man with heavy eyelids and chalky skin sat with his back against the metal wall. The room's single light shone down on him from above, illuminating the same metal cockroach nestled in his thick black hair.

"Yeah, America. Where you from? China?"

The Asian man looked surprised. "Do you speak Chinese?"

"I can't even say hello in Chinese. So answer my question, are you from China or not? You speak English like you're from the States."

A scowl formed on the Asian man's face. "I don't speak English. Only Chinese." He reached up and tapped the metal cockroach. "To talk much and arrive nowhere is the same as climbing a tree to catch a fish."

Carter stared at the man a moment. "I know a few Chinese proverbs. Man who eat many prunes get good run for money."

A smile slowly spread across the Chinaman's face. Then he laughed from his belly. Carter had never heard a laugh quite like it before.

The Chinaman's laughter eased into a pleasant smile. "My name is Han, and I am a rice farmer. What is your name and what is your livelihood?"

Carter frowned. "Carter Stone. My job? I'm unemployed."

A flicker of recognition twitched in Han's eye. Either he had experienced joblessness before, or he knew Carter wasn't being completely honest in his nondescript answer. Han looked over Carter's shoulder. "What's *your* name?"

Carter turned at a sound behind him. The Russian was standing, holding his head.

"Nikolai Mironov," said the Russian as he looked about the enclosed space.

"And what's your occupation?" asked Han.

"Lieutenant in Special Purpose Forces," Nikolai replied with the same stoic inflection as before. "You speak Russian?"

"Yeah," said Carter. "You think we're dummies? Of course

we speak Russian."

"How's your Pashto?" a disembodied voice asked in perfect English.

Carter looked about, but only saw his two companions, and that same piano machine, which appeared contented to stay where it was.

"Who said that?" he asked.

"Right here." A man dressed in a black turban and loose-fitting robes appeared. "Anyone who's been with the Mujahideen long enough knows you never announce yourself to your enemies until you're sure, one, they can't kill you. And, two, you can do that to them."

"Three against one," Han said. "The odds are in our favor."

"Never underestimate your opponent."

With lightning-fast reflexes Carter didn't think possible, the Afghani grabbed Han and spun him around, his arm wrapped around his neck tight. His face began to turn red from the pressure.

A smile of satisfaction blossomed on the aggressor's face, as if to say he could kill him with a jerk of his arm.

Han put up his hands, as if to surrender, then kicked his leg straight up, hitting his opponent in the face. The Afghani stumbled back, momentarily stunned. With a calculated look in his eyes, Han knocked the man down with a flying kick, and then put his knee on his neck. "Like you said," Han retorted, "never underestimate your opponent." He got back to his feet and assumed a safe distance from the man who had attacked him moments before.

"Whatever we've gotten ourselves into," Carter observed, "it's going to be an interesting trip."

* * *

The twin suns bore down on Taliah as she walked the path from her home to the training grounds. The lavish, air-treated housing she'd been assigned would have made most men and women from her station in life extremely happy. For her, it made her feel the opposite. She was one of the few of her people from the planet Kor to have been given such privilege. While she dined on the food of the Overlords, the people of her world—her own mother and father—survived on scraps.

She was also sad, for if her world had remained undiscovered by the race of Overlords, she would have married Prince Torvix. Then she would have been lifted out of her lowly position as a hunter of game designated by her people's caste system, to that of a Princess of the Eight realms. In that reality, a child might have been growing in her belly.

She often imagined this. Wishing it to become reality. But Torvix was dead. Killed in the war against the Overlords. She would have been executed alongside him if it weren't for her abilities as a fighter.

Her past was as dark as her skin. The village chief had insisted she take up the Art of the Blade, and indeed he had been wise, for it had saved her life against the Dergamin tribe when they raided her family village. And it was her swordsmanship that caught the eye of Prince Torvix, though he had liked to joke that it was her beauty that wouldn't let his eyes go.

All that was gone.

She was simply a well-treated slave now. And the luxurious food and housing would only remain as long as she continued to prove herself by training the incoming fighters.

And she hated it. Hated the killing, for its sole purpose was to give the Overlords tactics for future conquests. To train the Diremen, pale, soulless armies of genetically engineered killing machines grown at the massive incubation centers. With all the brains the Overlords had, they depended so much on their technology and on the mutated men they grew in the incubation vats. It wasn't just the Diremen they were constantly perfecting. The Overlords constantly worked at tweaking their own genes toward their definition of perfection, they seemed less like human beings, and more like machines.

They'd tampered so much with their genetics, blind spots had developed over time that normal human beings would have seen. As powerful as the Overlords were, their greatest strength—their brilliant minds—had become their greatest weakness.

Taliah watched the great walled edifice of the arenas grow larger as she neared them. The Overlord's world would have been beautiful if not for the twisted souls that ruled it. She bent down and picked up a blue flower with red tipped petals and put it to her nose.

Such a sweet smell. She tucked the flower into the tangles of her woven hair.

If she could find a way to rid this beautiful world of its sickness, she would give her blood gladly to the cause. There were others like her. Fellow slaves. And to her surprise, even a few of the Overlords.

It seemed even among the most twisted, genetically engineered race known in the galaxy, a soul designed to be cruel could be born with the defect of having a heart.

Not *everything* went according to plan on the Arena Planet.

That was a good thing.

CHAPTER 3

How long the four of them had been there, Carter couldn't say. Each man had declared a spot as his and expected the others to respect it like it was a sovereign territory. The same level of darkness permitted their eyes to see one another, but not by much. Mostly, they slept when they could. During their waking hours, cups of water would appear out of nowhere.

Was it provided by the piano machine that hovered above them like a hen watching over its chicks, Carter wondered? Or were there other creatures about, hiding in the darkness? Observing them? Looking for what? He had no idea. None of them did. They only knew they were here, wherever here was.

Something awoke Carter from a restless sleep. With no idea what time it was, the hours blended together into one long existence of monotony. Then, as though some force had taken over his thoughts, he looked up. Something had changed. The piano machine. It was gone.

"Get up," Carter said to his companions.

Like him, they spent most of their time sleeping.

"What is it?" Han asked. He rose to his feet and looked about. "Is there a problem?"

"I'm not sure."

"It's probably nothing," Nikolai said in an acerbic tone. "Americans do that, you know. You cause all kinds of commotion, and then retreat into the safety of your decadent culture. And for what? Just to let the world know you're there."

"Bigoted statements aside," Carter said, "would you consider the disappearance of our robot friend nothing?"

Both the Russian and Chinese moved into the middle of their holding area. It seemed his observation of what had happened wasn't good enough for them. They needed to investigate the matter themselves.

"He's right," Nikolai agreed after he looked about. "It's gone."

"Where do you think it went?"

At the edge of the shadows, Carter picked up on movement. It moved with slow, deliberate steps. "Something has changed," a low voice said. "In this situation, I do not believe that is a good thing." The Afghani stepped into the light, what little of it there was, anyway.

When he did, Han balled his hands into fists.

"Who made you the expert here?"

The Afghani stopped. "Expert, no. Suspicious, always. With the little information we have, unexplained events should always equate as danger."

A Russian, American, Chinese, and Afghani. Why were they there, Carter wondered? They didn't seem to have anything in common. In fact, they couldn't have been more different from one another if they tried.

The ship, vessel, whatever it was they were on shuddered underneath their feet. All four men threw their arms out to keep their balance.

"What was that?" Nikolai asked, fear edging into his voice.

"How am I supposed to know?" Carter asked. He wished he did know. He wished a lot of things about what had happened. But like the others, he only had questions and no answers.

A low rushing sound reverberated off the metallic floor. Intermittent at first, the sensation started at Carter's feet, and rose through his body. The longer the sensation lasted, the stronger it became, and louder.

"Whatever this is," Nikolai said, "I don't like it."

"Quiet," Han rebuked him. "Those things unseen can be just as informative as what is seen."

Carter thought it a profound statement, but next to useless. What they needed to do was work together and fight against whoever had abducted them. They could get philosophical with each other later.

"I think we're slowing," Nikolai concluded

"How can you tell?" the Afghani asked.

"The vibrations," the Russian replied.

Carter realized Nikolai was right. "What do you think it means?"

"We're here," the Afghani said in an emotionless tone.

As the words slipped past his lips, a ball of light appeared. About the size of a man's head, it hovered above them for a few seconds, and then grew in size and intensity. When it did, the same rushing sound as before returned, only, much louder this time. Little by little the decibel level increased, causing an intense throbbing in Carter's head as it did. His only defense against this sonic weapon was to put his hands over his ears, but it did little good.

All four of them fell to their knees, their clinched teeth an indicator of the pain each man experienced. Consciousness slipped away from Carter, and everything went dark.

A heavy hand rammed into Carter's back, followed by a quick jab to his ribs.

"Move!" a low, guttural voice commanded. Whatever it was, it spoke English, though something about the creature's tone didn't sound quite... human.

His head still pounding, Carter looked about. What was this place?

Through his haze, he detected movement ahead, but couldn't make it out. It might have been the three other men who had been abducted with him. On the other hand—

The same voice as before barked into his ears, tender as they were, "I said move!" The creature rammed something into his back, hard.

An electric shock shot through Carter's body. No, not a shock. Excruciating pain ignited every nerve ending in his body. He gasped and grabbed his stomach as searing white heat shot through him. Carter braced his legs to keep from collapsing. If he fell, he suspected it would be much worse for him.

"Don't resist," a voice said from behind. It sounded familiar, and friendly.

Carter turned to see Han. Though they barely knew each other, he was never happier to see a familiar face in his life. "What is this place?"

He pointed up.

Carter followed his hand. A cave-like structure fell into view. Angled upward at a forty-five degree angle, jagged rocks of browns and greens disappeared into the darkness above. The roof must have gone up hundreds of feet, if not higher, though he couldn't be sure since he couldn't see where it ended.

Down below, where he found himself, dozens of people stood in a single line. All appeared to be human. Some of them looked Asian, while others were as white as he. A large number, however, seemed different. He couldn't quite say why. Their skin color wasn't quite the same as what he'd seen in the multi-ethnic city of New York. Or the way their hair looked, if one could call it hair. Some had hair as fine as the fur of a dandelion. For others, it was firmer and thicker, like it had been made of wood. And their faces. Many of the noses were longer than he had ever seen, and the people taller. Some of them must have been seven feet at least.

Where was this place?

"Just keep walking," Han encouraged him. "As long as we cooperate, we should be okay."

The creature with the same guttural voice rammed a long silver pole with a glowing orb on the end into Han's back. He winced in pain, but didn't break his stride.

"No talking," the creature growled.

So much for cooperation.

As they walked, Carter noticed the only sources of light were glowing balls imbedded into the sides of the cave. All around him, grunts and groans sounded, either from the inflictor of pain, or the inflictee.

The creatures that carried the pain sticks kept a wary distance from every man in line, their arms outstretched to inflict punishment for the slightest infraction at a moment's notice. They were tall like the others, though their faces were hidden by a metallic mask contoured to the angles of their faces. Just two slits indicated where their eyes were. They also wore what looked like body armor that banged and clanked with each step, a constant reminder of who was in charge.

The only thing Carter knew for certain was that he had already grown tired of getting prodded with their pain sticks. The first chance he got, he'd take a swing at one of those things, and let him know what men from Earth could do.

"Don't even think about it," a familiar voice said. This one, though, was different. Deeper, and without emotion.

The Afghani glanced back over his shoulder. "You make a move, and it can be bad for all of us."

How could he have possibly known what he was thinking? "What are you, psychic or something?"

"Not psychic. Attuned to my environment. Your steps have gotten short and choppy, and your breaths have become forced, like you're preparing for something. I suspect either trying to escape, or attacking one of our guards."

"You figured that out from steps and breaths."

"No talking," the guard creature ordered. This time, mercifully, he didn't use his pain stick.

The line went through the cave until it entered a long corridor. Made of the same kind of rock, smaller spheres lit their way. Even if Carter thought about escape, it wouldn't do any good here. The walls pressed in on them little by little the further they went. Because of their height, the taller members of the group were forced to bend down. A few misjudged the distance, and banged their heads into the ceiling more than once. If their situation wasn't so dire, Carter would have thought it was funny.

A small opening and adjoining room appeared at the end of the tunnel. A four-armed humanoid dressed in vestments reminiscent of a priest stood in the middle of it. Light in color they were, and covered with a strange-looking embroidery that cast a hypnotic spell on him. As each prisoner approached the priest creature, he held out his arms and said in a monotone voice, one that suggested he had said this hundreds of times before, "May the deity you believe in protect and watch over you." The creature turned his attention to the prisoner after him. "Next."

At the end of the widened area appeared another doorway. Unlike the one they had just come through, this one was filled with light. One by one, the prisoners were herded through it. Was this the end, Carter wondered? If it was, he wasn't going down without a fight. They may kill him for his disobedience, but he would at least have the satisfaction of knowing he took a few of his oppressors with him.

As Carter stepped through the lighted opening, a miles long bridge extended into a massive plain stretching out to the horizon. Three suns located in different corners of the sky illuminated a number of structures dotting the plain. They were oval in shape, and tall. Several stories high by his assessment. Arenas? He did a quick count in his head. Sixteen of them.

"Move," the same creature with the pain stick ordered him.

Just where had he been brought?

The closer they got to the first arena, the more Carter didn't want to know.

CHAPTER 4

A small, square-shaped platform extended out from the bridge used by Carter and the others. The closer they walked toward it, the more it appeared the square wasn't actually attached to the side. It just hovered in the air, hundreds of feet above the arena. A little further ahead, a woman with long sticks held in her hands slowly came into view. Like the other people he had seen, she wasn't exactly human. Human-like, but not. She was as tall as him, with long slender arms. One could say every part of her was slender. Even her hair. Waist-long strands of gray and violet fluttered in a soft breeze. It gave her a lithe quality he found attractive. If they were on Earth, he might have asked someone this pretty out on a date.

"You stop here," the same growl as before ordered him.

Carter knew by now the consequences for disobeying a command.

To his surprise, Han, Nikolai, and the Afghan were singled out as well. Not only them, but four other men in line in front of them. They were guided to the other side of the bridge. He spied a similar looking platform and woman also holding long sticks. Except, they weren't sticks. Guns would be more of an apt description. A metallic barrel, wood stock, and at the front end of the weapon, what looked like a bayonet attached to it. What was going on?

"I am Taliah of Axinar IV," the woman on his right said in a trim voice, every syllable enunciated with perfect clarity. "If you do as I say, you may survive the first round."

"Survive?" Nikolai asked.

Carter looked over his shoulder at the Russian. His narrow eyes and stony face were fixed on her.

"Yes, survive." She pointed across the bridge with long, nimble fingers at the other four receiving the same instructions. "Those are your opponents."

"Why are we here?"

"To win, of course," she replied cryptically. She spun the guns around so the stocks faced each man. "Each of you take one. These will be your only weapons in the arena. Use them well. Remember, you only have one shot, and then the blade will be your last defense."

Carter took his, as did the others. Was this some kind of joke? He wasn't a historian or anything, but he knew a flintlock when he saw one. This was the late 21st century, and he had been given a weapon two centuries behind him.

"And if we refuse to fight?" the Afghani asked.

"Then you will die, and your planet will be enslaved by the Overlords." She took a step to her right and motioned for them to step onto the platform.

Carter had had enough of this. Game time was over. "You mean we're supposed to fight to the death down there?"

His challenge registered in her eyes. They seemed to glow as violet-grey as her hair. Her mouth turned downward, as though she relived a bad memory, but it only lasted a second. Taliah's stoic demeanor returned, and she pointed at the platform a second time.

"There is no clock or time period. You take as long as you need to eliminate your opponents, and they for you. When there is a winner, that team will be taken out of the arena and brought to its cage."

Death. Fight. Cage. None of this sounded good, and it certainly wasn't imaginary. He was here with those taken from who knew how many other worlds, perhaps moments away from death.

As they stepped onto the platform, Carter looked over the edge. The arena sat directly below them. In the open area, he observed what looked like green grass and trees. Dotted amongst them, small white squares. What they were, he couldn't quite see at that height. What he could see was a large, gray ship not far away from the elevated bridge. It also hovered above the arena. For what purpose, he could only guess. An observer ship perhaps? Small portholes dotted the side. Underneath, what looked like advanced cameras that scanned the area below.

Carter no longer thought of the arena as such, but had become a stage in his mind, and they were the show.

"May the deity you worship watch over and protect you," she said before the square descended.

"We don't have much time," Han said, who had been silent until now. "But this does seems like a test of some kind. If we don't work together, we'll fail it."

The Afghani held up his gun. "I have never used anything like this before, but that doesn't mean they can defeat me. We Mujahideen have a long tradition with the sword. It is a weapon of honor."

"One shot or a hundred," Nikolai boasted, "I'm not worried about our opponents. I gave them a long look, and it seemed like they couldn't tell one end of the gun from the other."

"Have you learned nothing?" Han chided him. "Never underestimate your opponent." His eyes drifted in the direction of the Afghani.

"Unity," Carter said, "that is how we overcome our enemies. In the business I was in, it has kept the people I worked for in power for decades." His boss. Carter had sworn to himself he'd never kill again. Fate, it seemed, had other ideas.

The platform landed hard in a grassy area. Where the other platform landed, he couldn't tell. Han kept sight of it a hundred yards or so away, until it disappeared behind a row of trees.

They jumped off it and formed a loose circle. Every movement made by them was observed by the armored ship several hundred feet up.

"Keep your eyes focused," Nikolai ordered them. "They could come out of the forest at any time."

"Not likely," Han said. "If they made a direct charge at us, it would be a simple matter of gunning them down. More likely, they're taking up a defensive position somewhere, hoping we'll make the same mistake."

Nikolai slapped the end of his gun on the ground. "How is it you know so much about them, Chinese? You a spy in our group or something?"

Han shook his head. "No, not a spy. A former lieutenant in the People's Republic Army."

"I'm an ex-submariner in the Russian navy myself."

Then it all made sense to Carter. They weren't chosen at random, they were picked for their particular fighting skills. In Nikolai's case, strategy and stealth. The Afghani, a mountain fighter. For Han, an officer and leader of men. In his own case, a hitman for the Escobar drug cartel.

"We should find cover," Carter suggested, "or this fight will be over real quick."

The Afghani pointed toward a low rise. "That way."

"Why?"

"Because I thought I saw some structures in that area. Just as important as defense is protection from the elements. How cold does it get here at night?"

"Is there even a night?" Carter asked.

"If you have another idea, then I suggest you offer it now."

All four men looked at one another. When no one said anything, the Afghani marched out ahead of them, his rifle held tight in his hands.

Carter had seen enough war movies to know the importance of keeping low. The taller the target, the easier it was to hit. He scrunched down and hugged the ankle-deep grass, his shoes making a swishing noise with each step.

Halfway up the rise, the Afghani got on his hands and knees and slowly made his way to the crest, the others doing the same. At the top, they looked down into a grove of green bushy trees. In the middle of it, three houses with peaked roofs, windows, and front doors stood in a row. A perfect line from what Carter could tell.

"What do you think?" he asked.

"No sign of movement," Nikolai observed. "It looks safe."

"Keep close and your eyes peeled. The other team can be waiting inside for us."

"If they are, they have a clear shot on us all."

"Remember, we only have one shot each ourselves."

Han reached down and picked up a stone. He threw his arm back and flung it with all his might. The stone arched into the air, and bounced off the side of the middle house with a loud clack. When it did, all four men planted their faces onto the ground. As the seconds passed, silence met them back.

After a minute, Han got back to his feet. "If they were there, we'd know by now."

Han's strategy was simple but effective in Carter's mind. The other two didn't say either way. At least they didn't object.

The Afghani assumed the lead position and went down the back side of the rise, all of them looking about, waiting for any sound that tipped off their opponent's location.

When they had gotten within twenty feet of the center house, the Afgani stopped and looked it over. "It appears—"

A sharp crack pierced the sky. Carter flinched, thinking he had been shot. He checked himself out, but he seemed okay.

"What was that?" Han asked.

The Afghani just stood there, then fell to the ground. A large red stain filled his shirt.

"Get to the house," Nikolai yelled.

Carter took off first, followed by the other two. He jerked the front door open and took cover behind a large box in the middle of the floor. As he did, another shot flew through the front window and lodged into the wall behind him. He was tempted to fire back in return, but that would have been a waste of his one and only bullet.

Han came in next, followed by Nikolai. He slammed the door shut and took up a position next to Carter.

"What should we do?" Nikolai asked between heavy breaths.

"I'm pretty sure that Afghan's dead."

"Now we know this arena is real," said Han, "and the consequences that go with it."

"Of course it's real," Carter snapped back.

Nikolai grabbed Carter's shirt. "This bickering won't get us anywhere. They now have a one man advantage over us."

"But we have a two shot advantage." Carter pointed at the hole in the window.

"No," Han replied. "One shot. The other gun is still out there."

Carter's anger boiled over. "No one thought to pick it up? That's just great."

"Pardon me for not wanting to get killed," Nikolai said in a sarcastic tone. "You heard what that Taliah person said, "'The number of people alive is what counts. Not weapons.'"

"Without weapons, you only have dead people."

Carter let the matter drop. They were in a bad situation, and fighting with each other wouldn't get them anywhere. What they needed to concentrate on was their next move. Those alien fighters were out there somewhere, and they had the advantage of knowing where their enemy was. Would they wait them out? Attack? Neither option sounded good to him.

"We're sitting ducks in here," Carter said after some thought. "If we wait long enough, we know the other side will come for us."

"That is what I'm hoping for." Han rose to his feet, careful to keep out of the line of fire from the window. He looked up and studied his surroundings. "Yes, I think this will do nicely."

"What are you talking about, Chinese?" Nikolai said, the same measure of disdain in his voice whenever he used his nationality as a pejorative. "You want them to come?"

"It's not a matter of want. It's a matter of reality. A mathematical principal if you will." He pointed at himself. "Three enemy opponents. Two bullets. The only way to get us all is with a direct attack. But we have one thing they don't."

"And what's that?"

"These houses. These flammable houses."

Nikolai let out a hot breath. "I think you must have hit your head when you landed inside. You burn these houses with us in them, and we're dead. How will that get us the victory?"

"Have you ever seen a fire?"

"Of course."

"It's mesmerizing. People can't help but stare at the flames as they crackle into the sky. Now, if you set three houses on fire, it will be like a magnet for our friends out there."

Carter was beginning to understand Han's plan. Only, one thing didn't make sense. "Nikolai is right. We'd only have minutes in here if we set this building on fire. The other team simply waits us out and lets the heat and flames do their work."

"Only if we're inside." Han went to the edge of the window and looked up. "The first sun has already set, and it looks like the other two aren't far behind. Maybe an hour or so. When it's dark, we get the first one going, and then duck out the back and hide behind some trees. The other team will investigate what's happened. When they do, that's when we attack."

Like Han had guessed, the second and third suns slipped past the edge of the arena and slowly made their way toward the horizon. As they did, the sky's greenish tint turned a deep shade of purple. Soon, it was so dark it became difficult to see one's hand in front of their face.

"How do you propose we start the fire?" Carter asked.

"That's the easy part," Han replied. He brought up his weapon and pulled back on the hammer. Held in place by a simple screw, he pulled out small piece of flint. "That's how these guns work. The flint strikes this curved piece of metal, which causes a spark, and ignites the powder."

"You're going to waste one of our shots?"

"That's not what I said. One of the bayonets should work just as well. All we need is a piece of cloth, and getting the fire going is easy."

"Will this do?" Carter asked. He cut the lower part of his shirt off with the blade provided by their trainer person. Crumpling it into a small ball, he put it on top of the box.

"Is there any paper or other flammable material in here?"

Nikolai and Carter looked about the room. Except for the box, they didn't see anything else.

"Nothing but walls and a ceiling."

What he said stirred in Carter's mind. "Walls." He went to the one nearest him and placed his hand on it. It felt smooth, and papery. Then an idea came to him. He rammed his bayonet into the wall and twisted it. As he suspected, a kind of wallpaper came off with each jab of the blade.

"Get as much as you can," Han ordered.

This was a command Carter was happy to follow.

Within a few minutes, he had a whole armful. Now he regretted tearing his shirt. They had more than enough paper to get the house going.

Carter took the flint from Han and then detached his bayonet. He had seen it done on a television show some years ago, so he had a sense about how to strike the flint with the blade. It only took a few passes before a small ember ignited the paper. A dull red glow formed in the middle of the pile, accompanied by a billowy shaft of smoke. He gently blew on it, which brightened the glow. Three puffs of air later, the paper ignited. Nikolai tore more strips from the wall and fed the flames. The box it was on soon started to smoke.

The three took a step back and let the growing blaze do its work. They watched the tendrils of fire reach higher and higher, until they licked the angled roof above.

"How long should we wait?" Carter asked. "If they see the fire before we're ready—"

"Good point," Nikolai interrupted. He went to the back entrance and started to smash it with the butt of his rifle. The door withstood the first few blows before chunks of wood splintered apart. The planks slowly disintegrated against the repeated strikes inflicted against them, until he had enough pieces that would serve his purpose.

It took a quick minute before they too were burning in the fire. Nikolai was careful, though, to keep one end out so he could safely pull the wood from the flames.

As the room burned, the amount of smoke increased. It soon became difficult to breathe. Han grabbed one piece of wood, Carter the other. Their guns held in their other hand, they peered out the back to make sure it was safe. Not seeing any movement, one went left, the other went right. Several broken windows later, the other two buildings were soon burning.

Carter, Han, and Nikolai darted into the woods and took cover behind three nearby trees, their weapons pointed in the direction of the massive bonfire.

"If this doesn't work," Nikolai whispered, "then we're in a

whole lot of trouble."

"We were in trouble the moment we woke up on that ship," Carter commented.

The sound of a foot swishing in the grass sounded on their left.

Carter didn't know about the others, but his heart lodged in his throat. He dare not make a sound or risk giving away their position.

Another footstep soon followed.

Were all four of them together, or had they divided up? The answer came when two men, both of them tall, appeared at the edge of the woods, no more than fifty feet away. They slowly approached the burning houses, their guns at the ready.

"What should we do?" Carter whispered. "I only see two of them."

"They must have divided up."

Han brought up his weapon and took aim. Nikolai followed his lead. A small click sounded when Han pulled back on the hammer.

"Remember," Carter said. "You only have one shot each."

With a steely gaze, Han zeroed in on his opponent. The hammer fell, ignited the powder, and with a loud blast, sent the ball into the chest of his target. The man's gun went off as he fell.

Before his teammate could react, Nikolai dropped him with a shot.

"Come on," Nikolai yelled. "Let's grab their guns before the others do."

As Carter rose to his feet, a musket ball struck the tree just above his head, sending small splinters into the side of his face.

Carter instinctively turned around and came face-to-face with another member of the enemy team. His opponent loosed a high-pitched scream, then came straight for him. Fumbling for the trigger, Carter swung his weapon around and fired without taking the time to aim. Either it was dumb luck, or some greater force had guided him, but the ball found its target, and the man flew back and landed on the ground with a dull thud. Dead.

"Have you seen the other one?" Nikolai called out.

Turning in different directions, Carter looked for any sign of movement. In the dark, that was all but an impossibility. The orange glow of the fires helped, but beyond a certain distance, a curtain of black surrounded them. Then, in the corner of his eye, he picked up on movement. Carter held his place, and then lunged at it. The last member of the enemy team jumped up and thrust his weapon forward. Carter dove out of the way, just barely missing being rammed through by the man's blade. He took a step back, and tripped on an unseen object in the dark. In the process, his gun fell out of his hands.

The man rose above him and raised his weapon. "Prepare to die," he growled, and then stiffened.

A small dot formed in the middle of his chest. The glint of metal danced in the fire light. The man looked down at the blade sticking through his shirt, its surface red with blood. Surrounded by profound silence, the man dropped to his knees, a distant look in his eyes. Behind him, Han held his rifle, his bayonet still in the man's back.

Not until he fell over did Han yank it out. Though it pained Carter to see a man killed in front of him in such a gruesome way, he also felt relief that his life had been saved.

Nikolai reached down and helped Carter up. "You okay?" he asked.

"A little bump on my head, but I think I'll survive." He turned toward Han. "Thank you."

Before he had a chance to answer, the arena was filled with light. The same platform as before appeared above them. It lowered onto the ground not far from where the three stood. They stepped onto it, and slowly lifted into the sky. Waiting for them in the same spot on the bridge where they had departed, Taliah stood with her hands clasped together.

When Carter, Han, and Nikolai stepped off of it, she nodded at all three. "It seems the deity you worship has indeed watched over you. Well done."

It wasn't about deities for Carter. Not even luck. They had used their cunning and skill to defeat an opponent who was just as determined to kill them. But it wasn't enough. The Afghani was still dead. Not only him but their opponents. What were their names? Did they have families at home? As a matter of survival, Carter and the others had no other choice. Still, he didn't feel much like celebrating.

"So, does this mean it's over? We won, so we return to Earth now?"

Taliah let out a chirpy laugh. "I'm afraid not. This is only the first round." She pointed in the direction of the other arenas. "You must defeat every opponent in these games if you have any hope of returning home."

Carter's gaze dropped, and he said as a sincere prayer, "God help us all."

CHAPTER 5

Taliah scrutinized the men she had been assigned as she stood in front of their cell. Their ability to band together and fight as a unified team, despite their obvious differences, more than surprised her. When she first saw them get off the transporter, one glance told her they wouldn't make it anywhere close to the final-round. But they had proven her wrong. With a quick victory achieved, they at least had a fighting chance, not that it would be easy. Han was as thin as a wisp of grass, and Carter looked like an average humanoid, nothing special, though his profile said he was a killer. Nikolai was the only man who had some muscle to him. Didn't matter how much promise the fourth man showed. With his death, he became a nonconsideration the second his heart stopped.

Of the four, it was Carter who surprised her the most. When she'd first seen him she connected his appearance to the profile sheet provided by the Overlords. Killers were usually the most unpleasant men to work with. Violence was their only positive trait, but they often made mental mistakes, such as letting their emotions get the better of them. If she had learned a singular truth in the arena, it was that you always thought with your head, never your heart.

It had been the Overlord's custom of choosing the worst kind of murderers from their home planet, and she had assumed Carter was no different. His face had looked like that of a killer when he arrived, but now it had softened, taking on a kinder, even attractive demeanor. She had been especially surprised at his reaction when she told him he would have to fight his way to the top if he ever hoped to return to Earth. He had mumbled some sort of prayer. Killers didn't do that. Not any she had ever seen, until today.

Her eyes scanned each man's face on her side of the polymorphic screen. It surprised her they hadn't tried a clumsy attempt at escape yet. So many of the first-timers did. Its translucent facade gave the appearance nothing stood between them and the outside. But on those occasions when they did try, those unfortunate souls got the shock of their lives, much more than the jolt sticks used by the guards.

"This cell will be your home for as long as you survive on the Arena Planet," Taliah said in the no-nonsense tone she used for new recruits. She laughed in her head. Recruits. More like fodder for the killing machine. "You will be fed well and your stay made as comfortable as possible."

"You call a cage comfortable?" Nikolai chided her from inside the cell.

"Let me tell you a little about the Arena Planet and how it works," she continued without missing a beat. "The Overlords are the most advanced civilization in the galaxy. They have destroyed upwards of a thousand worlds, and have enslaved twice that number. They've mastered genetic engineering, and have tweaked it to their advantage. Not one Overlord you'll ever meet is what I would call natural. Their genetic makeup has been altered again and again, and will continue to be altered as they upload new information into their artificial intelligence receptors. And that is partially why you are here. The Overlords want to maintain their dominance over every civilization they encounter. They are always hungry to find new methods, new fighting skills, and new strategies. Every arena battle you are in will be observed by Overlords. The mechanism attached to your brain is feeding them detailed information about your thoughts, your emotions, the chemical balance of various triggers firing in your mind. When you are in the heat of attacking an opponent this device sends them a constant stream of signals beyond just your heart rate, but your thoughts, your ability to handle the pressure, and the way the wiring in your brain either helps you win or causes you to make a fatal mistake. The Overlords will assimilate any advantageous traits they find in you and upload them into their own minds."

"Gladiators," Carter said. "We're like gladiators from the Roman Empire. But unlike then, this isn't for sport. It's for the purpose of maintaining their dominance in the galaxy."

"If that doesn't disturb you," said Taliah in a whisper, "nothing will."

Han said, "Clearly, it seems to disturb you."

"More so every day," she said softly.

"If this information is what they want, then why are you training us?" asked Carter. "It seems to me the advantages we'd gain for ourselves would taint the results of each conflict."

"I have been selected by the Overlords because of my ability to fight. My people were subjugated by them a generation ago. We are slaves, and as such my people serve at the pleasure of our captors. This is the price every world pays who is conquered by them. That is unless you win. But even then a tight rein is kept over your planet. You are free in one sense, but in another you are still a slave to the Overlords."

"And what if we lose?" Nikolai asked.

"You'll be dead, and things on your world will be made very much worse. Trust me when I say, victory is a far more pleasant outcome than defeat."

Carter said, "So you're here to help us?"

"Yes," said Taliah. "I will be training you as long as you survive each round in the arena."

Nikolai came within a hair's breadth of the poly-morphic screen. His genial disposition slipped into a scowl. "You didn't give us much training this morning when we fought. Why didn't you help us then?"

A good question, one she had been wondering when they'd ask. "The first fight always takes place without a trainer's intervention so we have a purer idea of your fighting skills," Taliah replied. "And I must say you did very well. Three of you are still alive. But don't get too comfortable in your victory. Mistakes were still made that could have made the results very different. Such as all of you going into the center home together. If the other side had worked better as a team, and realized what you had done, they could have easily cut off your only means of escape and attacked your position. With nowhere for you to go, the fight would have been over in minutes."

"But we're still here," Nikolai said, his tone filled with condescension.

"For now. Of the thirty-two teams that fought this morning, sixteen have been eliminated. Of the sixteen remaining teams, only one survived without a loss of combatants. A few consist of a survivor or two. You have a strong chance against one of these teams, though you never take anything for granted. I have seen more than once a lone combatant win the competition for their planet. This is why it is essential that you bond together to bring down your enemies."

"Do we always fight with muskets," Carter asked, "or do they change things around?"

Nikolai grabbed Carter's arm. "I can't believe you're asking this she-creature here such a question. You've accepted the situation, and you're just going to fight?"

"What other choice do we have?" Carter replied. He turned back toward Taliah. "What happens if we refuse to fight?"

"Those who don't are killed, and the surviving members of the team are sent into the arena without replacements."

"Does that answer your question?" Carter chided Nikolai.

The Russian returned to his bunk, silent.

"As to your previous question," Taliah continued, "there are sixteen arenas in all, each with a unique landscape requiring different tactics to win. In the next match, for example, certain skills you possess should work in your favor. Nikolai's profile states that he once worked on a submarine... some sort of a nautical machine my own world never developed the technology for since our water comes in solid form."

"Great," Nikolai complained from the back of the cell. "She's supposed to train us how to fight, and she doesn't know what liquid water is."

"The grasshopper can never fly until it spreads its wings," Han said cryptically.

"What is that supposed to mean, Chinese?"

Han knelt and picked up a small stone and held it in front of

Nikolai. "See this. Round, smooth, hard. It exists as something created by natural forces."

"Yeah, so?"

"If I wrap my hand around it and throw it at you, this rock becomes a weapon." Han did just that, hitting Nikolai in the chest.

"Ow," he said. "You trying to pick a fight or something?"

"Not at all. I am trying to make a point."

"What point? All I'm hearing is crazy Confucius talk."

"You never know the ability of something until you see what it can do. This woman here has undoubtedly witnessed hundreds of battles in the arena. Her level of experience and skill goes far beyond what we know. I suggest we learn what we can from her if we have any chance of coming out of this alive."

"Well spoken," Taliah said. Clearly, this man thought with his mind. Nikolai on the other hand, she wondered if he would survive the next round.

"Your upcoming match is largely water-based, which is what we will train for. The water arena is bordered by land and the large body of water is sixty feet deep at the middle. Both teams will be given five different boats to choose from. As a team you can choose if you want to split up into three separate boats or remain together on a single one. Like everything else in the arena, each boat has its advantages and disadvantages. Unfortunately, that is as much as I can tell you."

Nikolai spat. "Of course."

"When you arrive in the arena you will have to make the decision based on your own judgment. I'm sure Nikolai will be crucial in helping make this decision. But let's talk about what we do know. The border of the water will have turrets spaced three-hundred yards apart. Any ship that approaches the land will be fired upon by them, each one equipped with a large machine gun mounted on top. Depending on what type of boat you have, the machine gun might not be effective, or it might rip your vessel to shreds."

"Wait," Nikolai objected. "If there's a vessel that has a long distance weapon that will give us an advantage. But now I have a question for you, Taliah. Are the turrets destructible like the house we burned down earlier today?"

"So nice to see you involved now," Taliah said with a hint of irony in her voice. "Everything is destructible. In some arenas you can set an entire forest on fire, or burn down a specific structure."

"Sounds glorious," said Han.

"Minus the part about dying and killing," Carter observed.

Taliah scrutinized him. "Your profile says you are a killer for a family of criminals, but the way you talk doesn't fit your profession."

"I've killed a lot of people," said Carter. Regret tugged at his words. "If the Overlords had come and picked me up a week ago, I'd have been a different person. I guess you could say I grew a heart. I *snapped*, in a good way." He smiled at her.

Taliah felt something in his smile. Something pleasant inside. In the years she'd served as a trainer for the Overlords, the only smiles she ever saw were sneers or crude grins in response to foul jokes. Carter's smile was warm and genuine. It had been a long time since she saw genuine emotion with kindness behind it. But that would not serve her well. More than likely he wouldn't live longer than one or two matches. She couldn't grow attached to these men in any way, no matter how different they were.

Han said, "So how many teams have you trained?"

"More than I care to count," said Taliah. "Forty, maybe fifty."

"And how many of these teams went on to win the entire competition?" asked Nikolai.

"Six," Taliah replied. "I am tied with one other trainer for second place. First Place goes to Zelroth Klin of Tatos Prime. He has fourteen victories. He is the oldest and most adept of the trainers. But don't lose heart. I've been here only twenty-one years. I have defeated his teams many times. But most of that will depend on you. Are you ready to begin your training?"

The men all nodded. She didn't tell them they would be going up against the other trainer with six victories. His name was Galonaun. And she didn't tell them that Galonaun was the trainer with four surviving fighters, but she would have to, for strategic purposes. The danger was if she disheartened her men before the battle, it could take on devastating psychological effects. She'd reviewed the video footage of Galonaun's fighters. Two of them were killers like Carter, one was a soldier like Nikolai, and the other man was an eight-foot-tall monstrosity that had single-handedly won them their first victory, killing three of the four men on the other team.

She looked at her three fighters. Somehow they already looked beleaguered. "Your next match will be a difficult challenge. What I am about to tell you may sound like the odds are not in your favor, but listen to me—victory is possible, but only if you follow my instructions without question, that and Nikolai's knowledge of naval warfare. If you do, you will make it through tomorrow's match, together and intact."

Nikolai returned to the front of the cell. He studied her before he said, "Alright, I'm in, but only because you need my skills."

"Let's begin."

CHAPTER 6

Carter looked at Nikolai's finger on the map a second time.

"Do you think they'll expect that?" Carter asked, his tone uncertain.

"No," Nikolai replied in his usual bravado, "and they won't see the rope from the shore. One of you two will be out there with me on the waters in the boats, and we'll tow that third boat. They won't realize we've left a man... as long as we don't bring the ships too close to shore."

"You're sure they won't all take to the sea?" Han asked.

"None of them are trained in nautical warfare. They'll be using the turrets on the shore and maybe a boat or two. If any are stupid enough to use a boat, I'll destroy them."

"I'm impressed," Taliah complimented. "Something so simple as a rope to win the battle. Just be ready for surprises. Things rarely go as planned."

Carter watched Taliah turn and look at him, then Han. "So, which of you will be the one who stays on shore?"

"Han should," Carter suggested without hesitation. "I saw his hand-to-hand skills in person. I'll drive the second boat."

"A wise choice," said Han. "My hands *and feet* are my greatest weapons. The men I kill won't make a sound."

"All right," said Taliah, "It's settled. Tomorrow morning we'll follow this plan, and only improvise when circumstances require it. I suggest everyone get some rest. Your match begins at the first sun's appearance."

Carter turned toward his bunk, which was no more than a small wood frame and a thin couple of blankets that could barely pass for a mattress. He felt a hand touch softly on his back.

"Can I have a word with you?" Taliah asked in a whisper. "Follow me."

Was this protocol, or something different?

Carter followed Taliah out the door, past several creatures with pain sticks standing guard in front of their cell. She led him down a small hallway, then stopped and looked about. Carter did the same, wondering what she was looking for. He didn't see anyone in the corridor. Taliah quickly opened what looked like part of the wall, which was in reality a hidden door. She grabbed his hand and pulled him inside. Her fingers were warm to the touch, and smooth.

When she shut the door behind her, darkness enveloped them. Were they in a room? Someplace larger perhaps? Carter extended his arms, but thought it best if he stayed put. No use bumping into something in the dark or stepping over a ledge.

"I am concerned," said Taliah, releasing his hand. "You seem hesitant to kill. Have I judged correctly?"

Carter stared into the darkness where he thought her face was. "First, why have you brought me here?"

Taliah looked about her surroundings, what Carter surmised she could see of it in so little light. "It's a place of refuge when I choose to be alone."

"Are you the only one who knows about it, or do other trainers use this place?"

"That's not important." Her voice bore a scolding tone that amused Carter. "My question is."

"Like I told you, I had a change of heart about killing."

"Tell me more of this," Taliah requested. Her voice held an empathetic tone. Not the harsh, inflexible drill sergeant they had known the last few days, but a female from another world who genuinely seemed concerned about him.

Carter gave her request some thought. Why did it matter to a trainer who cared no more about them than the other teams that had once been under her charge? She had one job to do—give them the skills they needed to win this contest of theirs. What did his feelings about killing matter? On the other hand, it was an innocent question, and she was probably curious.

"I worked for a man named Carmen..." He hesitated, realizing she likely wouldn't understand. "I'm sure things are different on your world, but—"

"You can speak plainly and not worry about me misunderstanding you," said Taliah. "We all have a translation device implanted in our brains. It also conveys the meaning you intend."

"I see." Carter continued, "Carmen is a criminal, what we call a drug lord. When someone got in his way or threatened his business, he needed someone to knock them off. Kill them. That was my job, and I did it for many years. Not too long ago, I was sent to kill a man named Clarence. He hid himself away in a church, a place where we worship a supreme being we call God."

Her eyes drifted downward, then lit up. "The all powerful one. The creator of everything. Yes, I understand."

"I thought he was just dodging me, but it wasn't like that. I would go in, sit in the pew, and watch and wait. There were al-

ways too many people around, so I'd leave after a while. This
went on for two days. I'd sit there in the pew, waiting for an opportunity to close the contract on him, but then the strangest
thing happened. Something began to eat away at me. Clarence
kept his eyes closed almost all the time. Praying. He was actually
praying."

"We have that too on my planet," Taliah interrupted. Her
voice sounded hurried, like she felt excitement about sharing
that particular piece of information with him. "Do you honor the
world builder as we do?"

"I suppose. We call him God."

"I'm sorry. I interrupted."

"That's alright." He rubbed his hand over his chin. "None of
the other men I had been sent to knock off did anything like
that. They always seemed crooked, or at the very least they tried
to run from me. Somehow that made it easier. But Clarence just
sat there, praying all day long. At night, after the church closed, a
priest would take him into a back room where he could get some
sleep. I didn't know what to think about this, but it didn't matter.
My boss was putting increasing heat on me to get the job done."

"Heat?" Taliah asked. "Why would he make you hot? To
motivate you?"

A soft laugh pushed out of Carter. "I guess that translation
thingy needs some work. Heat is an idiom. We also call it slang.
It means he was putting pressure on me. So on the third night I
broke into the church resolved to put a bullet in Clarence's head
and go back to life as normal. But walking through the sanctuary
that night, I felt this darkness inside me. Every step I took towards his room, it was like my feet got heavier. By the time I'd
reached his door I was crawling. I felt so heavy. Like my soul was

sick. Somehow I managed to open the door to his room. It wasn't locked. Who doesn't lock their door with a drug lord after them?" he asked rhetorically. "When I looked inside, I was on my hands and knees. There was Clarence praying under the light of a single candle. He looked up at me, saw the gun with the silencer attached gripped in my hand. I saw compassion in his eyes instead of fear. At that moment something broke in me—or healed, depending on how you look at it. That happened a week ago and ever since then I haven't had it in me to kill. Not until last week, anyway."

Carter waited for Taliah to respond but she remained silent.

"You still here?" he asked.

"Yes," Taliah replied, her voice filled with emotion. "I'm sorry. I haven't heard tenderness like that in years. Working here as a trainer, we're only given the darkest, crudest, men and women to work with, and the Overlords are no better. Your words touched me in a way I haven't been touched in a long time. They remind me of my people and my world. Prayer. Heart. Compassion. Things long forgotten on the Arena Planet."

Carter reached out and felt Taliah's arm. He stepped towards her and pulled her into an embrace. It had been a strange need, to comfort her. He had heard the pain in her voice. For a moment she lay her forehead against his shoulder and put her arms around his back, but then she jerked away.

"No," said Taliah "There can't be any emotional attachment between us, even if it's just friendship. I can't worry about you dying. And you... you must find a way to kill again. To kill for your teammates, and all the people of your world. You must become a savage again, just for the duration of these games. Then you can let your heart change."

Carter knew she was right. Any qualms he had about killing had to be put to the side. If he didn't fight, his teammates stood a poorer chance of winning. But far worse, if he didn't fight, what would happen to Earth and all the people on it, good and bad? Taliah had already warned him. They would be enslaved.

She took his hand in hers. "The Overlords, they are the ones who we must direct our anger towards. Ultimately we must..." Her voice trailed into silence.

"We must what?" asked Carter.

She squeezed his hand. Her fingers felt so delicate entwined in his.

"Maybe later," said Taliah. "For now just know you must kill."

Carter let out a heavy breath and he kicked the ground. "This is hard. Really hard."

"I know, more than you'll ever know."

"Okay, I'll do it," said Carter. "For my teammates and my world. But what about the Overlords? You've already said these games are designed to enhance their fighting ability. Are we not ultimately adding to the destruction of other civilizations?"

The door suddenly swung open. Hallway light poured in upon them. For Carter, it felt more like a searchlight, and they had been found out. A guard appeared, a pain stick in his hand.

His eyes widened when Taliah stepped forward. "Protocol violation seven. You should know better than this," the guard growled in a low, guttural voice.

She bent forward. "No disrespect intended. He and I had a private matter about the upcoming engagement. Your masters wish a good fight, do they not? Our conversation addressed that very issue."

It wasn't exactly the truth, Carter thought, but close enough.

The guard bared his teeth. They were straight, and sharp, like vertical daggers ready to strike. "I'll pretend I didn't see this," he snarled. "Taliah, you should be more careful." The guard took a step back.

"We need to go," said Taliah.

Not until they went around a corner did Carter release a breath he didn't know he was holding. "Why did he let us go?" Carter asked. "When I saw that stick in his hands, I thought some pain was coming my way."

"Not now," said Taliah. She passed through the door of his cell and peered outside. "It's safe. No guards here."

She pulled Carter by the hand. Once inside, her only words were, "Get some sleep." Not until she left did he breathe in deeply. Something was going on between Taliah and that Overlord guard. Some kind of understanding. Then his thoughts turned to the morning's battle.

His chest stirred with emotion. Han would do the killing. Carter simply steered the decoy boat. He would not have to kill this time, but that was only if things went according to plan.

CHAPTER 7

The cold breeze whipped Carter's hair as the platform lowered into the arena. Han and Nikolai stood on either side of him, their faces cut like stone. The smell of saltwater—the same smell as the New York Harbor—stung his nose. But this sea was no ocean, rather more like a medium-sized lake. In the far distance he watched the other platform lower with three thin figures and a large bulge that must have been the giant Taliah had warned them about.

"I see the boats," Nikolai observed. "This is turning out better than I hoped."

As soon as a platform landed, Carter and the other men hit the ground running.

"That large ship with the mounted machine gun on top, that one's mine," said Nikolai. "Carter, I want you in that strange spherical ship with the guns sticking out. That large barge-looking boat with the huge cannon, we'll tow that one."

Carter thought his ship looked like a silver porcupine that had the ability to shoot missiles out of its ass. He wondered what kind of world a strange-looking boat like this might have come from. Perhaps it was from their opponent's world. If so, they might know a few things about the vessel that they themselves were ignorant of.

Han took off down the shoreline staying among the trees, disappearing behind a thicket of ferns.

"First thing we need to do is find the rope," said Nikolai. "We secure it to the sphere ship and then head out. As we sail into open waters you have to play with these guns, figure out how they work. Just be careful not to blow me up, got it?"

Carter couldn't decide if his question was a warning or a threat. "I'll try not to."

They found the rope quickly enough. It was spooled in one of the smaller ships they would leave behind. The two worked together and hauled it out. In less than a minute they had connected it to the aft section of the spherical porcupine ship, which had already been connected to the bilge.

"First thing you need to do is figure how to steer that thing," said Nikolai, urgency in his voice. He scanned the other side of the lake. Like them, their opponents had boarded the largest boat available. Firepower, it seemed, had been the preferred strategy of both teams. "Once you have a handle on that and fire off some shots, I want you to follow my lead. You're my rearguard and my protector in case they attack from our flank."

Carter thought he could handle that.

The side of the sphere ship had a circular hatch that Carter slipped into. Inside, the red glow lit metal scaffolding had a distinctly alien feel. Carter moved up to what he thought was the front of the ship, but it turned out to be a hold for storage. He quickly rifled through it and found it loaded with stacks of different kinds of weaponry, such as translucent metallic cubes that resembled grenades and small arms that were spherical and strange. Carter grabbed one of the guns and followed a spiral glowing staircase that went upward. When he reached the top he found himself in what looked like the command center. A huge window stretched across the entire top. Dials and buttons just as strange as the inside of the ship blinked and glowed with different colors and sounds.

Carter approached what he thought might be the control panel and was shocked to find the instrumentation was labeled in English, and to his surprise, Russian and Chinese. The Overlords were making this as fair a fight as possible. Or so it seemed.

Drawn toward the control panel, Carter placed his hand on a lever that looked big and authoritative, and pushed forward on it slowly. An engine in the back of the ship growled, and it began to move forward. He peered at the distant horizon of water on the opposite side of the lake. It appeared that two enemy boats had already pulled out of their harbor. In front of him was Nikolai's ship, no more than thirty feet long, but decked out with a huge gun on top. Nikolai flashed him a grin and waved for him to follow.

Feeling the thrill of the chase, Carter moved the huge lever forward at incremental clicks. The spherical ship roared as it charged through the waters, creating a massive wake. He glanced down again at the controls. Large white labels practically jumped off the console: weapon one, weapon two, weapon three, all the way to weapon thirty-four. This thing was outrageous.

He randomly chose weapon twenty-one and pushed the appropriate button. A toggle control craned down from the ceiling. It had a grid with a target pointing straight ahead. He carefully aimed it away from Nikolai's ship and activated the only button on the toggle, a big red one. The ship shook and a deafening blast sounded. The sky suddenly lit as a huge fiery ball pulsed out from the sphere and came onto the grid. Text scrolled just above the display top that read, "press to explode."

Carter waited five seconds, counting them off in his head, then did as instructed.

A blaze of light illuminated the horizon. Carter couldn't help but smile. The ship was badass.

He clicked on weapon number four, his favorite number. Another toggle fell from the ceiling. And with it, another grid and another red button. The only difference was that the grid had some zoom function, and the text scrolling above it said, "Use your voice to zoom in or out."

Carter said, "Zoom in."

The device panned forward quickly, and he directed it using the toggle to move towards the enemy ships. Slowly, the ships came into view, until Carter's sights were almost upon them.

"Stop," said Carter.

The zoom stopped. He looked at both ships; one of them identical to his own, except its command center was no longer protected. Somehow, the top of the sphere had been removed and the command center lay exposed in the open air. A chill ran up Carter's spine. Standing at the helm was the giant. A toggle had already been lowered over his large face, with one eye staring out. It almost felt like he was looking at him. Something like a broad grin stretched across his opponent's face. Smoke issued from a large gun in front of the sphere.

"Oh crap!" Carter shouted. Before he could say anything else, the back end of Nikolai's ship exploded in a ball of fire.

Taliah's warning had come true. Their plan had gone to hell before it had even started.

* * *

Han moved quickly among the bushes. The boats could move much faster than he, and so the sooner he got to the enemy the better. There was something strange about the jungle at the edge of the water. It crawled with lizards and bugs, though none he had ever seen before. What was the point of the insects and reptiles? Were they there just to make it feel more real? Like an authentic jungle from their home world? He had a bad feeling it was more than that.

The booming of the ship's weapons snapped him back into the game. No, not a game. The fight for their lives. An even larger explosion stopped him in his tracks and he quickly made his way towards the beach. A column of black smoke drew him to a small outlet. From there, even from that distance, he watched in shock and surprise as the Russian's boat slowly sank, its fiery wreckage floating and billowing smoke. Had they just lost Nikolai? If so, perhaps it was better he went back for one of the smaller boats.

No, Han realized. He had to take out the turrets. It was their only chance. Hopefully, Carter could make do on his own.

A soft breeze brought with it a strange smell, faint, familiar. He turned at the same time a crash sounded behind him. Leaping from a thicket of ferns was a large Bengal tiger. He had only seconds before it would reach him. He steadied himself.

"You are the Dragon," he said to himself, and took off toward the tiger at a dead sprint.

* * *

Carter quickly maneuvered the crosshairs onto the giant ship as it approached at a high rate of speed. Though he had never remotely fought in this fashion before, he found himself enamored with the idea of a distant kill. Less personal that way. His thumb came down hard on the red button. His ship shook, and Carter's breath caught in his chest. If this didn't work, all that giant had to do was swivel his weapon in Carter's direction and he was as good as dead.

The view screen suddenly lit up in bright light. The spherical ship the giant had ridden upon had taken a direct hit, and was now engulfed in flames. Through the toggle grid Carter viewed the giant still standing on the bridge filled with fire and smoke.

Suddenly, it seemed to become too much for him, and the giant leapt from the ship and dove into the water. Carter moved the toggle aside for just a moment to gauge how far the enemy ships were.

He swore. The second ship bore down on him like a ramrod, no more than fifty feet away. He braced himself for a collision. When the ship struck, Carter found his body tossed against the base of the weapon's panel. The top of his own ship collapsed and the shockwave, caused as a result, struck him at full force. Like his opponent's vessel, smoke billowed from the front of the hull. In front of that was the enemy ship where a man stood staring at him from the deck, a gun in his hand.

Carter rolled just in time as shots spun off the metal frame of the control panel. He twisted down onto the deck, using the control panel as cover. He drew the gun he had retrieved from the storage room and stood. Wrapping his finger around the trigger, he fired wildly in the direction of the shooter.

The man fled for cover as Carter continued to shoot. He

wondered how many rounds he had in his weapon. It wasn't shooting bullets, but some kind of energy beams. Did beams run out?

His years as a hitman taught him that you never stayed in one position for too long, or your opponent could turn the tables and come after you. You always took the fight to him. Taliah had pointed out as much after their first time in the arena. With those thoughts in his head, Carter jumped onto the top of his boat and slid down the smooth metal sides, landing on the deck of the enemy ship. At his approach, the man fled into the cabin, and Carter pursued him. It was then, Carter picked up on a trail of blood. Though he didn't act like it, the man had been hit. He reminded himself to proceed cautiously. Wounded animals were always the most dangerous.

Carter stepped carefully into the smoke-filled hallway. With his weapon extended, he found a cabin door at the end of it. Locked, as expected. He drew in a deep breath and kicked it open.

The man lunged at him from the darkness. Carter fired, but just missed the side of his head as he slipped under Carter's guard and hit him at full force. The man drove him hard against the ship's decking and the two began wrestling for control of the gun. Carter twisted and rolled the man over onto his back. He tried to rise to his feet, when the man kicked the gun from his hand. The weapon skittered along the deck, coming to a stop a dozen feet away. The man grabbed Carter by his leg and twisted, spinning him to the deck again. His opponent lunged for the gun, but Carter stopped him when he grabbed his legs. A kick to the face dislodged Carter.

The man dove for the weapon a second time. Carter grabbed

him by the waist and knocked him hard onto the deck. A heavy grunt gurgled out his throat. They slid a few feet, to a naked part of the railing. Below, water slapped the hull. Carter's hands were wrapped tight around the man's wrist that held the gun. As they wrestled for it, shot after shot passed Carter's ear. Both of them now hung over the railing, the wind whipping over the lake battered against Carter's head. Below, he picked up movement in the water. At first, he thought it was a large shark gliding along the water's surface. But then, to his horror, he realized it was the giant as the man climbed from the water onto the anchor and chain attachment, using it as a ladder.

Carter had little time. Without that weapon he knew he was a dead man.

He drew his free hand back and swung his fist at the man's face. A soft crunch told him he had broken the man's nose. Crying out in pain, he dropped his gun, which Carter grabbed. Six shots later, the laser blasts fired into the man's chest at point-blank range had done their work. The fight in the man's body stilled, and he slipped from the deck and fell into the water below.

Despite his adrenaline, Carter felt something dark inside him, something he hated. He had just taken another life, and there was at least one more life he needed to take before this could all be over.

He looked back down at where he'd last seen the giant climbing, his gun ready to fire. A massive hand swatted the weapon away, breaking it into pieces. Carter cried out; his hand felt broken. The giant climbed onto the deck and Carter could only backpedal as the creature approached. He was looking at death himself. The giant somehow looked inhumanly ugly. The thing only had one eye, and a huge head set upon a thick muscled neck that rested on barreled shoulders. The sight of him up close made Carter's knees weak.

But then he saw something behind the giant, something climbing onto the deck.

It was Nikolai, as wet and haggard as a half-drowned drunk.

A smidgen of hope returned.

* * *

Han rolled the limp tiger carcass off of him and onto the ground. A huge tongue stuck out of its mouth between razor-sharp teeth. Han tried to stand then dropped to a knee. The tiger had taken a chunk out of his leg, and his chest felt like the animal's claws had nearly pierced his heart as they had racked against his ribs like precise cutting tools, leaving exposed skin.

Despite the pain, Han tried to stand again, clenching his teeth as he did. Slowly, he managed to move one step at a time towards the turret. Near the water's edge he found plants that were native to his own country. Medicinal plants. He scooped up some of the leaves and placed them on his raw wounds. They might help.

A turret boomed in the distance. He looked out at the water, smoke billowing from a large collision. He couldn't see the figures, just the smoke. Whatever happened out there was beyond his control, but the shore was his hunting ground.

The first turret he came upon was a large stone structure. Slowly, painfully, he hobbled up the steps. What he saw at the top stopped him in his tracks.

Below a large machine gun were two boots sticking out from

the mouth of a bizarre looking creature that was half lizard, half snake. A massive man-shaped bulge bloated the front of its body, much like a snake with a rat lodged in its mouth. The scary thing about this creature was that it had legs. How fast it might move Han didn't know. Fearful the lizard snake might come after him, Han slowly backed down the steps. At least the creature had provided one beneficial service: it had eliminated a member of the enemy team.

Not far away, the sound like a rapid machine-gun fire caught Han's attention. Another turret. He grimaced and moved forward again, the pain in his leg and burning of his chest a reminder that if he should encounter another jungle animal, he would soon be like the man on the turret. Food.

* * *

Carter would've been dead already if Nikolai didn't have a gun. As they stood now, Carter was further away from Nikolai than he would have liked, and far too close to the ugly monstrosity. The only thing keeping him alive was Nikolai's line of fire. Nikolai had a straight shot if the giant should lunge at Carter. But Nikolai was unable to move, pinned down by turret fire, just like Carter. Blast after blast continued to tap and splinter the deck siding above Carter's head. Everyone was held down but one, the man in the turret. And the giant wasn't staying idle. He kept his one eye fixed on Carter—the other eye appeared to have been badly maimed in some form from a previous fight, maybe even in the arena.

The giant slammed his fist repeatedly against the wood deck, trying to punch a hole through it and get below deck. It appeared his determination and strength worked in his favor. The colossal man must have weighed five hundred pounds at least, and he'd successfully pulverized a huge chunk out of the deck and was now yanking on wood planks and popping out nails by brute force. Carter had to do something. The last thing he wanted was that behemoth loose on the ship with a weapon.

Carter stayed low, keeping out of the path of whizzing energy bursts that continued to pop every few seconds. The turret gunner seemed to be hoping he'd make a mistake and peer up at the wrong time. Nikolai did what he could from his distant position, but the cross-fire proved an effective deterrent. Nikolai shook his head in frustration. Carter held his hands up as if to say, *Trust me.*

The giant peered up at Carter, his immense face sneering an ugly grin that seem to say in reply, *Come any closer and I'll take a few bullets just for the pleasure of ripping your arms off.* The look gave Carter pause.

He didn't like the idea of being bait, but he had to do something. Rather than let it happen, he moved closer to the giant, keeping low under the fire of the bullets. The giant peered up again, turning his attention away from the hole he was pounding in the deck. Some kind of grunting noise sounded from his thick purple lips.

"Do something," Carter ordered himself. The hole in the deck was growing larger by the second.

He suddenly jumped to his feet and rushed toward the giant. A huge face stared back at him, a glint of concern lining his hungry eyes.

The enemy on the turret intensified his attack against Carter in response. Tight energy bursts splintered the deck all around

him. He dove behind the railing and glanced back at his opponent.

Eyes wide, the big man ran straight at him, a high-pitched
scream filled the air. Carter lunged in the direction of Nikolai's
position and felt the swish of air behind him from the giant's
large hand. It was only then that Carter realized his mistake. The
ground shook behind him, and the giant used him for cover.

Ahead, Nikolai's face turned white as he stared down the
sights of a handgun, frantically looking for a safe shot. Nikolai
begin to backpedal while still aiming. He cracked off two shots
and then turned and ran at the same time Carter reached him.
Both of them ran toward the bow of the boat, the giant's feet
pounding violently behind them.

Nikolai turned back and fired as he ran. Several soft thuds let
Carter know the shots found their target. As he threw a glance
over his shoulder, a half dozen blue dots marked the creature's
chest, with what he assumed was blood. Unfortunately, it didn't
have the result either of them had hoped. Rather than slow the
brute, fierce rage filled his glaring eye.

"Over the side," shouted Carter.

Nikolai didn't have to be told twice. Both men jumped over
the ship's railing and fell, hitting the water awkwardly.

Carter began to swim with Nikolai. Thoughts of success at
their escape filled him with hope; they died in an instant when a
splash reminiscent of a large, fat kid at the community pool
landed near him. But the enormous splash hadn't been preceded by the cry of *cannonball!* Nor had the fat kid taken seven
or eight slugs to the chest. The man pursuing him could hardly
be called a man at all, but a cycloptic demon from hell; more
horrifying than Carter's worst nightmare.

* * *

Han gripped the metal handrail of the stairs to the last turret. He felt like his strength was almost gone; he wasn't sure if he could make it up to the top. Despite his exhaustion, the sound of the machine gun's blaring told him in no uncertain terms his teammates were desperate for his intervention. The medicinal leaves he found didn't feel like they had helped at all, and he questioned what exactly he would do when he reached the gunman above. Did he even have the will left to finish this?

A couple of quick blinks refocused his eyes. He squeezed the railing with the last of his strength. He had to try; the call of death was the only other alternative for him and every person he knew on Earth. Each step up felt like the tiger had ripped into his chest all over again. Just as bad, every heave of his lungs put pressure on his open wounds.

Somehow, despite the agony of each lurch forward, he made it to the top of the turret. He limped forward inch by inch as quiet as a swaggering drunk. The sound of the weapon going off multiple times a second covered his approach, and the man's attention was fixed on some apparent action in the distance.

Han reached him, swung his arm around the man's neck, his hand grabbing at his opponent's pointed chin. When he went to snap it, his silent enemy spun around and broke away from Han with ease.

For a moment the man looked at him wild eyed, at his chest covered in blood, skin shredded. Han stared back, his vision blurred, the world spinning. He suddenly fell over, dizzy. In that brief moment, the way the uniform fit his opponent, bumpy in places it shouldn't have been, he wasn't a man at all, but a woman. This changed everything. Could he actually kill a woman?

She didn't give him much time to think about it. Her face as hard as stone, she glanced back at the gun, then again at Han. She went to give Han a kick to the head with her heavy boot. Han's fingers reacted as if they had minds of their own, and sprang to save their owner's life and caught the woman's foot, then twisted, bringing his enemy to the ground.

Han lay there, every breath killing him a little bit more. His opponent recovered quickly and grabbed Han's boot. With a strong jerk against his body, he felt himself being dragged towards the metal stairs he had just climbed. The woman was going to throw him down its one hundred foot height. He envisioned his bones breaking with every thump of his body against each step, until the mercy of death met him at the bottom.

Just as he expected, she gripped Han's leg, and in one motion, attempted to heave him toward the stairs. It was the momentum Han needed. He hooked his legs behind his assailant just as he was about to be tossed over the side. The woman shouted in surprise as she found herself hurled along with Han down the stairs, only now Han had managed a tenuous position on top of her. His opponent landed hard on the angled steps as Han guided his knee directly under the woman's throat, the force of his landing dislodging the woman's neck bone from her spine, killing her instantly.

Han collapsed beside the dead body, sucking in air by the lungful. Cold, lifeless eyes stared back at him. Pangs of guilt tugged at his emotions. He wasn't proud of what he had done, but what other choice did he have?

As much as he wanted to stay and reconcile with himself the

ethics of his actions, Han forced himself back to his feet and again ascended the steps. He dragged his lame leg over to the turret machine gun and looked through the sights. It took him several long seconds to find Carter and Nikolai in the water, the giant swimming like a crocodile behind them.

Han fired a burst of rounds into their pursuer before the monstrosity sank beneath the waves.

From above came the sound of clapping when the observer ship came in low over the water. The Overlords. Han had forgotten they were even there.

As he looked up, the world around him slipped into darkness, and he collapsed onto the turret floor. It was over.

CHAPTER 8

"A most engaging resolution, wouldn't you say, Master Telmin-Kai?" Jelsik-Ryy asked, his half-human, half-reptilian face as stoic as ever.

Dressed in the appropriate attire for a second tier Overlord, Telmin-Kai never liked it when his adversary called him out like that in front of the other Overlords. It struck him as unseemly, and a little pretentious.

He pulled on his tunic as he rose from his observer chair. The view screen suspended in front of him lifted when he did. It had been a splendid match between the Earthers and those from the Fellyx system. In his mind, the right team won.

"Yes," he replied after drawing in a deep breath through his filter gills. "What I would expect from a second round engagement." His fighting boots clomped heavily against the observer deck plates. He kept his answer brief, so as to not give his opponent opportunity for an effective rebuttal.

"I find these Earthers quite resourceful myself." A trace of envy edged into Jelsik-Ryy's tone. "Not at all what you'd expect from a species that appears weak and ineffectual at first glance. I have not been surprised like this for some time."

In the corner of the observer deck, his back to the other two, the first tier Overlord, Sulit-Bay, spoke with the head representative of High Magistrate Raxon-Pal, one of his oldest and dearest friends. Telmin-Kai considered him a friend as well, if one could have friends in the Magistrate's inner circle. How many had thought of him in the same way, only to find themselves in disfavor for an innocent comment perceived the wrong way? Or worse yet, endured The Trials as a result of their questioned loyalty.

As they spoke, he wondered how he would do if he faced The Trials himself. Not a pleasant experience for all involved, especially the one accused. But they served their purpose. How could the High Magistrate maintain order over a hundred billion lives on countless worlds if those who served under him could not be completely trusted?

Sulit-Bay turned around, a smile swathed across his auburn-tinted face. His blue uniform made a swish sound after each step as he walked across the observer deck, his friend at his side. "Yes, I agree," the first tier said. "We will have to keep our eye on this one."

"Who?" Telmin-Kai asked, more than a little curious.

The first tier did not respond at first, his attention seemingly elsewhere. He clasped his gloved hands together, then said, "I believe his name is Carter... something."

"Stone," Raxon-Pal's representative filled in for him. He tugged on the part of his robe that had slipped down his arms. He pulled at it just so, tucking the edges inside the folds as the custom of his position demanded.

"Yes, of course. Carter Stone." The first tier scratched the side of his face. His double-chin jiggled when he did. "He shows promise, this one. I believe he can be the leader of his team if he asserts himself. So far, however, he has displayed his skills to my satisfaction."

"What about Menseratis from the Kohlani System? He alone killed three of his opponents after suffering what I thought was a fatal injury. His healing properties are quite remarkable."

The first tier considered the representative's words. "Yes, he too might reach the final round. His race has definite advantages over Earthers. They are bigger, stronger, faster, and can withstand a great deal of punishment. Though I find their strategies more on the one-dimensional side, nothing we haven't documented before. New skills and ways of fighting are what we're after. Not traits that are inherent in their physiology."

Telmin-Kai stepped between the two. He knew Raxon-Pal's representative took offense at the slight, but he didn't care. Nothing more than an opportunistic sycophant in his opinion. "I agree. Strategy and enhanced fighting skills are the purpose of these arena conflicts. And the Earthers have not disappointed. The applause we offered their victory is ample evidence of the respect given them by us. My report will analyze the strengths displayed by him and his confederates without bias, and their weaknesses as well, just as I've done since these matches began. There is one thing that concerns me, however."

The first tier's disks of valor blazoned across his chest glittered when the lights above hit them just so. Whether intentional or not, the effect enhanced his presence. "And that would be?"

"It is something that I've thought about for a long time now." He paused before continuing. The first tier had made it known he welcomed any and all suggestions and observations after every match, though his range of interest did not depart far from it. A challenge toward his policies, or those of the empire, might not be received well. He warned himself to proceed cautiously. "Have we grown too comfortable in our position as arena observers?"

Sulit-Bay let out a hearty laugh. "You have always amused me, Telmin."

Telmin restrained his emotions at the disrespect shown him. Sulit-Bay had addressed him by only half his name. If anyone else had, Telmin-Kai would have challenged him to personal combat. "In what way?"

"You worry about such trivial matters. These conflicts have kept the ruling family in power for eleven generations. I assure you, we are quite secure from any threat. Insulated I think is a better word."

"Have you not heard about the discord in some of the frontier systems?" Telmin-Kai asked in a sharp tone. "It's been said a number of their leaders have openly advocated secession from the Raxion Union."

The wispy representative tugged on his multi-colored robes. "Nothing but rumors and idle threats from those who would usurp the positions of their superiors. Talk such as this has filtered through the halls of influence and position since there have been halls. Yet, we are still here, and the arena matches provide us with the fighting skills and strategies that keep Raxion Union intact."

"A crack unmended can fell the strongest bridge," Telmin-Kai said.

The representative's slitted eyes narrowed. "I'm sorry, but is that supposed to mean something?"

"A proverb. It means any structure is vulnerable if areas of weakness are ignored."

A softer laugh escaped with the first tier's breath. "I believe these verbal matches between you two are almost as informative as those we observe below."

Sulit-Bay was right. Telmin-Kai didn't think much of Raxon-Pal's representative, and the same was probably true in reverse. Yes, it was true. Of course it was true. Why else did they spar with each other at every opportunity? In some ways, he supposed, it reinforced his position within the Magistrate's inner circle. Aggressiveness and self-confidence were highly prized virtues in their sphere of influence, so long as it did not undermine their principal belief of absolute loyalty to the High Magistrate.

"I stipulate that Taliah of Axinar IV should also be recognized for her contribution to the Earther's victory," Telmin-Kai declared.

Sulit-Bay spat. "The only reason she and her people still breathe is because of their intuitive fighting skills." His jovial mood disappeared under a dark cloud that settled over him.

A foolish mistake, one Telmin-Kai regretted immediately. It was at Sulit-Bay's insistence her world be made an example of two generations before when they openly revolted against the Raxion Union. Normally, it would have been blasted away by their retribution ships. But he was also right in pointing out their advanced fighting skills. It served the empire's purposes to let them live, but it didn't mean he liked it. Any mention of someone from Axinar IV, and the first tier took it as a personal affront to his good name. Never would he make that mistake again.

"You are right, of course. Though a defeated people, they should carry the yoke of subjugation and shame as long as one of them remains alive."

"Here, here," the second tier Overlord said, content to keep his thoughts to himself until now.

Sulit-Bay's cloud didn't lift. "As much as I enjoy this friendly banter between us, we all have some work ahead of us. I expect your analysis reports by the second sun's first light."

He offered them a quick nod, and then left the observer deck, Raxon-Pal's representative at his side.

The second tier came up to Telmin-Kai. "Yes, a most engaging conflict today, wouldn't you say?"

"I thought I already had." He spun and headed straight for his quarters.

CHAPTER 9

A flicker of light bounced off the cave walls. Normally, this deep in the tunnels, glow orbs were used for illumination, but even at minimal power levels their energy signatures would have been detected by the Overlord's sniffer drones. They weren't programmed for fire.

"I don't think she's coming."

A few paces ahead, Regin's brother, Telmar, stood at the edge of the shadows. Worry knitted his brow. "She'll come. She's the one who called us here."

Regin took a step toward him. "What if she's been found out? If they put the bore worms on her, I'm not sure she could hold out against the pain before they killed her. She knows everything about us."

"Taliah is stronger than that, and smarter. If she were ever discovered, which I doubt, they'd never take her alive."

"I don't know. It makes me nervous just being here. If we're caught..." His words faded.

A hint of a smile bent upward on Telmar's shadowed face. His brother had always been the nervous one, even when he had no reason. In the best of times, before the Union had conquered their world, he found things wrong in the family, or in the town, or their whole society. If they weren't brothers, he wasn't sure he would have put up with his doleful ways as much as he did. "Patience."

A stone in the distance skittered off the cave floor.

Both brothers froze.

"Who's there?" Telmar called out.

Regin grabbed his shoulder. "What are you doing? What if it's a sniffer drone?"

"If it's a drone, then we're already dead, and you no longer have to worry."

The hand on his shoulder tightened.

Both men listened in silence. What sounded like footsteps slowly approached.

Telmar held out his torch. From the wall of black, a hooded figure approached, alone. The person's hands were clasped together, a visible sign he was from their home planet of Axinar IV. Or she in this case.

"Taliah?" Regin asked. He took several nervous steps back, enough that his brother now stood between him and the stranger.

"I'm sorry I was delayed," a woman's voice answered. She pulled the hood off her face.

"Taliah," Telmar said. "It is good to see you again. When the team you trained in the previous arena cycle didn't make it past the first round, I thought the Overlords would have disciplined you."

She gingerly rubbed her shoulder. "They did."

A deep growl slipped past Telmar's clenched teeth. "One day they'll pay for what they've done to you, to all of us."

She stepped into the light. "Yes, but today is not that day."

"We don't have much time," Regin said after several nervous breaths. "Why did you summon us here?"

"You already are aware the Earther team has reached the third round. I believe they have the skills to reach the final match, and perhaps come out of it alive. More specifically, the one named Carter Stone."

"We've heard some stories about their victories, how they work well as a team, and have presented the Overlords with a number of innovative combat methods."

"Yes."

Telmar peered closely at her. "Do you think this Carter Stone can be the one?"

"I don't know yet," she replied.

Her voice didn't waver, and she kept her gaze fixed on his. She spoke the truth. Yet, something else lined her words. A hesitancy, though it wasn't about what she said. Something else underneath. Concern, perhaps.

"You must decide soon or everything we've fought for could be lost. The next arena match is in two days."

"Trust me, they'll be ready. You can be assured of that."

Regin grabbed Telmar's arm. "We should go. The sniffer drones can't be far off."

Taliah looked over her shoulder. "He's right. Every moment we delay is dangerous." She slipped the hood back over her head. "I'll contact you again when I've made my decision about Carter Stone. In the meantime, let our people know to prepare themselves in case our instincts about him are correct."

She turned and melted into the dark.

* * *

"No, no, no," Taliah yelled louder than their previous training scenario. She snatched the sonic gun out of Nikolai's hand. "This is a weapon meant for distance, not close range. The closer you are, the less effective it is."

The Russian jerked the helmet off his head. "Pardon me for getting it wrong," he sniped, "but I've never fought in the air before. These anti-grav packs are tricky. One soft bump on this poor excuse for a joystick, and you're tumbling away out of control."

"It's meant to be sensitive. Air pockets, changes in temperature, an enemy combatant that pulls up in front of you—if you don't maneuver out of the way quick, you're dead."

Han, who had been hovering in the air twenty meters up, reduced power levels for his anti-grav thrusters. He landed on the ground hard, but remained on his feet. He winced in pain when he did. "Nikolai is right. We're not accustomed to this kind of technology. Four days is not enough time."

Taliah let out a hot breath. "The match is tomorrow, and you're nowhere near ready. You don't know what's riding on this next round if you lose."

Carter thought it strange she put it that way. Since they arrived on this miserable planet, it had been all he thought about. His life, the lives of his teammates, Earth's future. What else could there be? "Are you saying there's more involved than our side winning?"

Hesitation seeped into her expression. "The only thing you need to worry about is tomorrow's match."

"Han's in no condition for this level of training. Look at him." He pointed at Han's bandaged chest and leg.

"The treatment he received should be sufficient. You're fortunate the physician didn't designate him higher than a level five damage status."

Carter wasn't sure what the significance of that was, though he suspected if the doctor had, it meant Han wouldn't face any more arenas in the future.

"I can still fight," Han declared in a tone that left no room for debate.

"We can all fight. What I don't understand is why you're pushing us as hard as you are. Every moment of daylight, it's nothing but drills, combat strategies, and equipment checks. You push us too hard, and it becomes counterproductive. Has that not occurred to you?"

"Nothing you need worry about."

Nikolai took a threatening step toward Taliah. "And that's another thing about this place."

The annoyance Taliah manifested edged into her tone. "Which is what?"

"The combatants we've faced during each match. The Overlords. You. Everyone around here is human. Or at least humanoid in most ways." He pointed in different directions. "Everywhere you look, it's people."

She sighed, "Yes, what of it?"

"Don't you find that a little strange on a planet that hijacks people from all over the galaxy? You'd think there'd be cloud beings here, and creatures composed of nothing but energy, or insect people. Where are they?"

The agitation in Taliah's voice dropped precipitously. "Oh, they're here. Just not here."

Nikolai planted his fisted hands on his waist. "What's that supposed to mean?"

Taliah pointed upward. "On different arena planets. Like kinds with like kinds. This way, the Overlords get a better idea of how certain species fight, rather than their differences working against each other."

"There is some logic in their approach," Han concluded.

His anger just as resolute, Nikolai spun around. "What? You siding with these Overlords?"

"No, not siding. Just agreeing with their methodology. When two relatively equal combatants are pitted together, that's where the innovation comes in."

Like a dog with its favorite bone, Nikolai couldn't let the matter go. He said to Taliah, "And what have they learned from us?"

She ignored the question. "Starting positions. I want you three one hundred meters above. Stay as one as you go forward, and then break at my command."

"Fine." Nikolai put on his helmet and strapped it down.

Carter did the same with his. Though simple in appearance, his helmet was a technological marvel he never thought possible. The thin layer of protective covering draped over the exterior not only protected his face from the blast of air as he flew forward, but it also displayed his altitude, speed, direction, weapon's status, and location of everyone around him. If the military at home got their hands on one, war on Earth would never be the same. A pained sigh slipped past his lips. If he made it home.

The three of them activated their anti-grav drives and accelerated upward to an altitude of one hundred meters.

"Okay," Taliah said through the helmet headset, "angle yourselves forward ninety degrees and fly in that direction until I give you the counter-order."

Carter, in the middle of the group, placed his hand on the control unit and did as she ordered. He rolled forward with the others and flew horizontally for about a thousand meters, when she ordered in his headset, "Break!"

Just as they had been commanded, Han darted away from him on his left, Nikolai on his right.

Up ahead, a black rectangle hung in the sky like the big fat target it had been designed to be. Carter brought up his weapon and fired at it. The rectangle darted to the left, easily avoiding the sonic wave.

"You must anticipate its movements," Taliah chided him. "A miss like that can cost you and your teammates their lives."

"How am I supposed to do that?" Carter barked back. "That thing can move in any direction."

"Precisely. That's why you must fire multiple shots, not just one. Let the machine do the guessing, not you."

"Alright, I'll give it a try."

Carter spun around and repositioned himself. He came at the rectangle the same angle as his previous run. Taking aim with his weapon, the device darted upward this time. When Carter adjusted, Han came down at it from above and unleashed a volley of shots. One of them went wide and hit Carter in the chest. Pain burst in every nerve-ending in his body. Both arms went limp and he tumbled past the rectangle.

"No!" Taliah yelled in his headset. "You flew too close. Greater distance is required if you don't wish to envelope your teammate within the wave. Try it again."

Try it again. That phrase went round and round in Carter's head each night he dragged himself to his bed. Something had changed in Taliah. This had become more than training. It had become personal.

The three went back to their starting positions and followed the same aerial path as before. When Taliah told them to break, Han and Nikolai flew off in different directions like before. Carter tracked their movements on his helmet display, though he noted how Han flew further out this time.

Both men swung around in a tight turn and headed straight for the rectangle. Carter aimed his sonic gun at it and fired.

The rectangle avoided the first blast, but took hits from Han and Nikolai.

"That's got him," Carter yelled over the helmet speaker.

As the words faded in Carter's ears, Nikolai came up from below him and fired a second time. The rectangle darted left. When it did, Carter peered close at the machine. For an instant, a strange sensation washed over him. Though it shouldn't have been possible, it felt like he could hear the rectangle process the multiple targets coming at it from different directions. And in that moment, he knew where it would go. He took careful aim ten meters below his target.

Nikolai fired his weapon at the same time. The rectangle dropped ten meters in an effort to avoid his shot, straight into Carter's sonic blast. It struck the machine dead center and it flipped over onto its side. They had won.

"Very good," Taliah congratulated them. "That's the kind of shooting and teamwork I've been talking about."

Though she didn't offer her praise often, Carter took some satisfaction they had done something right in her eyes. What he didn't understand was why her approval meant anything to him.

"Form up at the starting point," she said in the same dispassionate tone as when they started. "This next round, two evader drones."

CHAPTER 10

Water dripped from a crack in the ceiling and plinked on the ground every ten seconds, just as it had done since Carter, Han, and Nikolai had been assigned their cell. At first, it was all Carter heard at night, other than the rhythmic snores of his two companions. But as the nights went on, and the fatigue factor in him grew from the rigors of training and combat, he found the water's clock-like precision helped lull him to sleep over time, like a kind of white noise machine people used in big cities.

Except, this night Carter couldn't sleep. Something about tomorrow's match felt different.

"You awake?" Nikolai asked.

Carter didn't respond at first. Since landing on this miserable planet, he didn't have much time to himself, a big part of his life he cherished back in New York. Every waking moment here was spent with his teammates, if one could call them that. Taliah, of course, who pushed them harder after each round. Only at night did he have a moment's peace in his own thoughts.

"Yeah," Carter finally replied.

"Can't sleep either, huh?" Nikolai rolled over on his mat, his stubbled face lit by moonlight.

Correction, Carter thought. Not one moon, but three. He still had to remind himself how different things were on this planet, wherever this planet was.

"No."

"Probably thinking about tomorrow. Do you think we'll beat them?"

The question had gone around in Carter's head the second they stepped in their first arena match, and it hadn't abated. In this place, it was either kill or be killed. Earth's future rested on this simple premise. Yet, the seven or so billion people who lived on his home planet had no idea their very existence was at stake.

"Kind of ironic."

Nikolai's eyebrows drew together. "What do you mean?"

Carter scooted up into a sitting position. He looked through the cell opening and took in a pair of crescent moons drifting toward the horizon. "Tomorrow. We're fighting for our lives, and everyone back home is blissfully going about their business, without an inkling of what's at stake if we lose."

"*If* we lose," Nikolai corrected him. "That's the key. We've done well for ourselves the first two matches. Only one person killed on our team. That Afghani guy, whatever his name was." He pointed at Han's sleeping form. "And Chinese over there. His chest and leg wounds, which are healing nicely I might add. I'm not worried."

"I don't know." Carter's gaze drifted downward, until it caught sight of a ten-legged insect that resembled a beetle; a bright orange one that moved across the cell floor in a zigzag pattern. "I guess you can say Taliah has me spooked. The way she's been training us for this match. It's like..."

Nikolai peered at him close. "Like what?"

"Like more is riding on our victory than moving up to the next level."

"Maybe she knows who we're fighting against, and the collective skills of the competition we'll be facing. Each team that wins faces one that's tougher than the last match."

"That part's true, of course, only... I can't shake the feeling something else is going on we don't know about."

Nikolai scooped up a handful of dirt and tossed it back down. "For me, there's only tomorrow. The same should be true for you and Chinese over there. Surviving to the next round is all that matters."

"He's right." Han rolled over and faced them both. He rubbed the sleep from his eyes.

A scowl formed on Nikolai's face. "Have you been listening to us the whole time?"

Several short chuckles preceded Han's reply. "Like I couldn't hear you. You talk louder than you realize." He struggled to his feet and went toward the cell entrance, stopping just before the shield that kept them prisoners. The moons' glows draped around him, imparting onto his form an angelic-like luminescence. "I'll be ready for tomorrow's match. What I need to know is will you be as well?"

"What kind of question is that?" Nikolai groused.

"Not you." Han turned and faced Carter. "If your head's not in the match, then we're dead."

Carter should have taken offense at the accusation, but he didn't. Han was right, as much as he hated to admit it. His head wasn't in tomorrow's fight, not all of it, anyway. He should know better. After all his years involved with organized crime, only the hit mattered. Not who the person was, or why he needed to be eliminated, or if he had a wife and children. The poor slob had crossed the organization, and the time had come to pay for his transgression. Tomorrow was no different.

"If you knew anything about my life, you wouldn't have to ask."

"But I am asking."

"Yes," Carter said in an elevated voice, "I will have a clear head tomorrow."

Han turned back and stared at the starry sky, both crescent moons now kissing the horizon. Carter's reply seemed to satisfy him.

Nikolai jumped to his feet and wiped the dirt from his pants and shirt, holey as they were. "If we're not going to sleep, we may as well get up. Can't be more than a few hours before sunup."

"I suppose," Carter said, content to keep his place.

"What do you think of her?" Nikolai asked no one in particular.

"Think of who?" Carter replied.

"Taliah. Any other hers you know of in this place?"

What did that have to do with anything, Carter wondered? Han's gaze remained upward, as though he hadn't heard the question, or thought it not worth responding to.

"Well?" Nikolai said a second time, his voice just as insistent.

"Fine, I guess, as far as drill sergeants go," said Carter.

"Would you consider her pretty?"

Carter remembered Taliah pulling him into the darkness of the hidden doorway. There had been a closeness there, and he'd noticed her attractiveness ever since that incident. But the arena battles and the need to survive overrode any soft or sensual thoughts he might have otherwise entertained. To him, only their survival mattered. Back on Earth, the way women dressed, or wore their hair and make-up, that caught his attention every time he walked down the street. But he never pursued women back at home. He was a hitman for the mob. Not many women went in for that sort of thing. So, he let them walk by and he'd go back into his apartment and lived his life alone. Not that he minded it. Solitude was a way of life that fit him rather well. As long as he had his books and movies, he had all he needed.

"Pretty, I guess in an alien kind of way. Hadn't thought about it much."

A sinister grin pressed on the corner of Nikolai's mouth. "I think she's worth spending a little time alone with, if you know what I mean."

Carter did, and it made him angry. Females, wherever they came from, were not things that were meant for conquests. They had thoughts and feelings and self-respect, just like everyone else. What a person gave was far more satisfying than what could ever be taken from them.

"I'll go along with pretty. Nothing more."

"That's the kind of talk that gets you killed in the arena," Han said, jumping in. "Focus is what matters. My master in Luen-Zhong stressed that more times than I can recall."

"You and that kung fu stuff," Nikolai chided him. He extended his hand and cut at the air with them in short, jerky strokes.

"I cannot tell you how insulting that is," Han said, his back to him. "My master could take your life five different ways just by looking at you. Students from all over China sought his mentorship. I was fortunate enough to be one of them."

"I know how much I appreciate your skills," Carter said. "It's helped us out in the arena more than once."

"It is not my choice to fight in the arena, but I'll do what I must."

"Arena. Arena," Nikolai complained. "All that's here is the arena. I'm sick of the whole thing. At tomorrow's match, I'm half-thinking of shooting at the ship that hovers over us as we fight, watching, scrutinizing. If we could bring it down, take out these Overlords, then we might get out of this place."

"A hand weapon against a ship that size, I hardly think it's possible."

Nikolai came alongside Han. "You never know until you try," he goaded him. "If you spent as much time thinking about escape as you did each match, then it might actually happen."

"It won't if we rush into a fight without a plan, just like you do. My master also taught me the importance of waiting, thinking, and planning. You must know your opponent better than you know yourself."

"Or blow your opponent away with a superior weapon."

Han shook his head. "You just don't understand. The Praying Mantis survives in his habitat because it knows when to wait, and when to strike. It has served me well in my younger days as a fighter." A tremor of pain twitched Han's face. "But that was a long time ago, and I'm a different man now."

Nikolai gave Han a shove. "Look at you. You just stare out at the stars, like it's a warm sunny night, without a care in the world. You talk strategy but I don't see you do anything about it."

Han slowly turned in Nikolai's direction, his face set like stone. "The whole time you've been shooting off your mouth, I've been formulating different types of attacks against our opponents. I do not think they'll be wasting their last few hours talking about how pretty their instructor is, or if she has some kind of agenda beyond us winning the next match. Only tomorrow matters. Nothing else."

"Who pissed on your breakfast?" Nikolai asked.

Had Taliah's increased demand for perfection gotten to him as well? Perhaps he was just as nervous about the match as Nikolai, and this is how it came out. Either way, this bickering served no purpose other than to divide them. And if he learned anything about this place, that was akin to putting a gun to your head and pulling the trigger.

"I think Nikolai's right," Carter said. "It's a few hours until sunup. Best thing we can do is get some sleep, or as rested as possible. The match will happen soon enough."

Han nodded and returned to his mat, as did Nikolai.

Several minutes later, their cell fell silent again, minus the drips of water that pattered off every ten seconds. Carter stared at each drop as it fell to the ground, wondering if he would still be alive at the end of the day.

* * *

Carter, Han, and Nikolai hovered in the air a hundred meters off the ground. On the opposite side of the arena, four aliens rose up to the same level as them. The air felt still at that altitude, and warm. Warmer than Carter would have expected. During their training sessions, the higher up they went, the colder it felt. Not here in the arena. It was hot, and was about to become even hotter in a few seconds.

Directly below Carter's team, Taliah waited, her hand covering her eyes from the brightness of the suns. She had given them her little pep-talk about not staying in one place for too long. As she put it, "A stationary target makes for a fat target."

As an assassin, he disagreed with her. How many hits had he made while positioned in a clandestine spot—in the shadows, behind a car, in the corner of a room—where his target walked into his crosshairs? Out in the open, though, a hundred meters up, no place was safe.

A high-pitched whistle pierced the silence.

The team of four across from them immediately flew off in different directions, then stopped. Just hovered there, like their thruster controls froze at the same time.

"Break left," Carter said into his helmet headset.

With a twitch of his wrist on the joystick, the directional thrusters in his anti-grav suit shot Carter in the direction of the arena's western wall. Though they had trouble with the maneuver during their training sessions, Han and Nikolai matched his timing within a fraction of a second. Like a single unit, they flew toward their opponent isolated from the others.

All at once, multiple sonic blasts came at them from the four aliens spaced equidistant apart.

In his helmet display, the distance between his team and the alien counted down. One thousand meters. Nine hundred. Eight hundred.

"We're going to have to take these guys out quick, or we won't last ten minutes out here in the open."

As the blasts came at them, the three bobbed and weaved around the lethal energy packets.

"Careful," Han said in Carter's earpiece, "I have a target coming around from our five o'clock position."

"Where again?" Carter asked. He checked his helmet display. Sure enough, the target on the right had flown along the arena perimeter and managed to get behind them.

He glanced back over his shoulder and caught sight of another member of the enemy team circling around in the opposite direction toward his position. From behind, they'd all be sitting ducks.

"I have an idea," Carter said. He spun around, but kept his momentum in the same direction. "Now I've got your butts covered."

"Five hundred meters," Nikolai called out.

Several bursts flew past them. Now that the other team had gone mobile, the shots were easier to avoid.

Taliah's words during their training sessions crashed into Carter's thoughts: *not too close, or your weapons won't be as effective.*

"At three hundred meters," Carter said, "open fire."

Though he couldn't see Han and Nikolai directly, Carter assumed they nodded their replies.

A sonic charge flew overhead, missing by a wide margin. Had he overlooked someone from the other side? Carter checked his visual display. Other than their primary target, the closest opponent still hovered a thousand meters away.

"No wonder he missed by a wide margin," Carter said under his breath.

"Three hundred meters," Han called out.

"Break!" Carter ordered.

Like a closed flower that bloomed in an instant, all three flew off in different directions. As they did, Carter brought up his weapon, followed by Han and Nikolai. Their opponent attempted to avoid the sonic blasts coming at him, but he didn't anticipate them all, and was hit in the chest as he attempted to fly upward. His limp body tumbled backward into the arena's southern wall. What happened to him after that, Carter couldn't say. He turned his attention toward the alien still coming at him from his left.

Though farther away than he felt comfortable, Carter took aim and fired. Like the previous shots that had come at him, his blasts missed by wide margins. His opponent fired in return. Carter tracked the blasts' trajectories on his helmet display, all five of them. He waited until the last moment, then darted up, down, left, left, and down again. Each blast detonated on the wall behind him.

"I've got one on my six," Han yelled into his headset. "I can't shake him."

Nikolai swung around and came at the enemy combatant at full speed. "Hold on." It was as though they were tethered together, the distance between them dropping down at a frightening rate. If he didn't pull up, the two would collide.

"Nikolai!" Carter called out.

At the moment when it seemed like neither could avoid the inevitable, Nikolai fired a side burst from his anti-grav unit, barely missing his opponent. As he did, Nikolai swung his weapon sideways and took him out with a single shot.

"That got him," Nikolai shouted in triumph.

Now the odds were in their favor. The importance of this wasn't missed on Carter. He caught up with Han and targeted the alien who had managed to keep his distance from them.

"For a level three match," Carter commented, "these guys are easier than I would have expected."

As the last word slipped out of his mouth, a sonic blast struck him in the arm. The world went black a moment as he tumbled away out of control.

"Carter!" Nikolai yelled. "Pull up."

Carter fumbled for the controls as he fought to remain conscious. Blood flew off in different directions as a level of pain he had never experienced before paralyzed his body. His right hand grabbed at the control unit. A push on the toggle slowed him, and he regained his bearings.

"Pull up or you're dead," a voice screamed into Carter's headset.

Images of the arena's walls were still fuzzy. He fired a long burst in the opposite direction he was moving. In his peripheral vision, a flat surface quickly approached. The arena's eastern wall.

"Pull up," he repeated to himself, and fired another long burst.

The wall passed underneath him by only a few meters. Finding himself beyond the confines of the arena, an immense plain stretched out before him. All it would take was an extended burst from his directional thrusters, and he'd be long gone. But for how far or long? The ship overhead stayed in its place, the Overlords no doubt tracking his every movement.

Carter fought off the pain, along with his desire to escape, and re-engaged the fight. He spun around and verified the position on his teammates, and the enemy. To his relief, Han and Nikolai were still in the game.

"Tactical," Carter said into his headset.

"I've just taken out enemy combatant number three," Han replied, "but this last one is tricky. I can't get close enough to get a clean shot."

"The one thousand meter guy," Carter said to himself.

"Let me try," Nikolai said, bravado tinting his words.

"No. Wait," Carter said, but it was too late. Underneath him, Nikolai shot forward in a burst of acceleration. His weapon at the ready, he fired several shots at the alien, but his opponent easily avoided the blasts. Rather than take evasive action, Nikolai flew in a straight line right at him. Like before, the alien held his place, not moving.

His strategy didn't make any sense to Carter, until he remembered the jobs he had done for his boss. Position yourself in a stationary spot until the target falls into your crosshairs.

Despite his useless arm, Carter fired his thrusters and came in behind Nikolai. Too late. The alien fired at Nikolai, hitting his anti-grav unit. A colorful explosion blew up the device, and he careened out of control toward the ground.

"I'm hit!" Nikolai yelled, and fell out of sight.

Han caught up with Carter, and the two flew toward the alien at full speed. He sat there ahead of them, not moving, as if daring them to repeat the same mistake as Nikolai. Carter could almost imagine the confident smile on the Alien's face, anticipating winning the match.

At three hundred meters, the alien calmly pointed his weapon in their direction. Counting off the seconds in his head, Carter said into his headset, "Break."

Carter flew toward his left, Han to his right. Rather than hold a linear direction, they curved back toward the alien. Letting go of the joystick, Carter brought up his weapon and fired as many shots as his trigger finger allowed. Han did the same a millisecond after him.

With greater finesse than Carter expected, the alien dodged the shots with relative ease.

"Who is this guy?" he asked himself.

Then, as though his enemy's thoughts filtered into his, his next move became clear in his mind. *Let the machine do the guessing, not you.*

Carter aimed downward ten meters and fired a single shot.

His opponent dodged several blasts that came from Han, then dropped his altitude ten meters, straight into the shot fired by Carter. It hit him square in the chest, and he slammed into the arena wall behind him. His anti-grav unit destroyed in the collision, he fell to the ground, a cloud of dust rising at the point of impact.

Unsure if the alien was still alive, Carter circled over him at a safe distance. But the creature never moved. A quick check on his helmet display indicated only two targets in the air remained, him and Han.

"That is how you keep your head in the game," Han said in an emotionless tone.

But what about Nikolai?

Carter scanned the arena floor. A figure that looked like Taliah bent over a darkened figure not far from where the alien had met his death. If Nikolai was dead, then that meant there was only the two of them, and he with a shot up arm. However this worked out, they were in serious trouble.

CHAPTER 11

Taliah hurried down the halls of the Overlords' Palisade. It was only her second time being summoned before council member of the high twelve, and she had a foreboding sense that what they had to say would require complete control of her emotions. The last time she visited the Palisade they had tried to prod her for any hints of the growing rebellion in the slave worlds under their control, and it had not been easy resisting. Not when they used their telepathic minds that could pull and probe at the shadows of meaning in every word one said.

The mother chamber was vast and complicated. Three levels high, going in either direction as far as the eye could see, countless small alcoves housed a mix of races who possessed skills in the administrative areas. Monitoring a civilization a hundred billion strong required beings with such abilities. Endless streams of data, reports, and news flowed in from every part of the Empire. Such vast quantities of information needed to be assessed and distilled into its most basic components for the Overlords to effectively manage the colossus they had created.

There were no stairs. Only lifter pods that activated when anyone moved within their pre-programmed sensor range. Ahead, she beheld the great tentacled lifter machine rising out of the floor, surrounded by a short line of Overlords awaiting an open pod.

A guard approached her with his shock stick.

"What's your business, slave?" His voice dripped with contempt, as it always did whenever they addressed what they considered as inferior species.

"I was questioned when I came in, need you harass me a second time?"

"I'll do what I want to a weak thing like you."

"Then you'll be answering to Arum-Ton." She handed him the electronic summons printed on a thin sheet of metal.

He looked at it and scowled. "Be on your way then."

Taliah moved up to the line, now only two bodies long. Why did Arum-Ton want to see her? Would he be alone? Would his questions revolve around the growing unrest of their slave worlds?

When her turn finally came and she stepped into the next pod, the egg-shaped enclosure sealed itself, then shot off with nauseating speed. The pod read the code imprinted on the metal card, and within seconds she decelerated and the hatch opened. What lay before her could not have contrasted with the chamber more. Taliah stepped into a lush patio garden. Water cascaded down a short rocky fountain that created a soothing noise amidst the flowery aromatic foliage. In many ways, it reminded her of her home on Axinar IV. How she missed her family.

A voice beckoned her from a pillowed chair.

"Ah, Taliah. Come join me."

Taliah moved toward the Overlord who reclined in his cushioned chair. Dressed in a blue uniform, as were all the males of his species of his position, his disks of valor blinded her a moment when they caught the suns' light. She blinked the effect away. When her vision cleared, she noticed drinks for two set out on a small table covered with an edible arrangement of food.

"Please sit, Taliah."

Like a good servant, she obeyed.

"So quiet. Please, you are my guest. Have some delicacies." His long eight jointed fingers reached out and scooped at a bowl of white pliable clusters that dripped some sort of juice as he raised them to his mouth and dropped them in. These she knew to be the eyeballs of an alien creature their race bred simply for their eyes. They found them delicious and addictive.

She again obeyed and took from another bowl with a food that did not disgust her.

"Taliah, you have served the Overlords faithfully now for many years. That is why I have called you here. You may not know this, but there are a number of council members who to this day wish we had never spared your world. I am of course not one of them." He sat up and studied her with great interest. More thoroughly than he had in times past. "Your people have provided us with important knowledge that has helped keep the Raxion Union in power these last three generations. We owe a debt of gratitude to your peoples' fighting skills, if a master can owe its slave anything."

"Thank you," she replied. "You honor me and my people." Gratitude was the last thing she felt. Contempt would be more like it. But if she shared even a hint of her true feelings, he'd probably kill her on the spot. Just as frightening were his thoughts, and how they probed hers if she let him. Though it took a great deal of effort, she had developed the skills necessary to keep him out. The day she didn't would be her last.

"Though your world is a slave world for now," he continued without breaking his thought, "I would like to propose to the Council that we release Axinar IV and make it a free world under our authority. The restrictions and requirements currently endured by your people would be greatly relieved. It is your faithfulness these last two generations, Taliah, that is the impetus for my putting forth this amendment. But those council members who still despise your people because of the trouble they cost us years ago will be hard to sway."

Arum-Ton tried his best to make his reptile-like eyes appear warm toward her. A vulture snake would be more like it, him and all his kind. Cold-blooded, heartless monsters. What race could possess a soul that enslaved others for their own benefit? Yet, his offer of amnesty appeared genuine. For the last eleven generations, she couldn't think of a single instance an Overlord voiced such a sentiment, let alone intended to act on it. Was this a trick? Did her response determine a terrible fate for her or someone else?

"As I'm sure you're aware, unrest exists on many of our slave worlds." A chortling sound squealed from his lips. A response she knew to be laughter, though it came off as more like a feral ground beast shrieking from an arrow wound.

"Why do you laugh, Arum-Ton?" asked Taliah.

"My people seem to have a fatal flaw in-built in us. Though we can conquer and fight like no other race in the universe, we have little desire to do other things required of sustaining a civilization. Rarely do we breed with one another." Again, the painful chortle repeated. "And the factories that produce our soldiers can't keep up with the number of worlds we take in each season. If the resistance should unite, we may not be able to keep them in check. We would be forced to destroy them with one of our retribution ships. A true pity, for each slave world provides important resources for expanding our empire. That is where you may be able to help us. In return, I may be able to help you and your people. The council members are moved by loyalty."

Taliah sensed where this was going. "What would you have me do, Arum-Ton?"

His head tilted to one side, as though he hadn't decided until that moment to reveal his naked thoughts. "There are conspirators here on this planet. They must be rooted out. Information is being passed to the resistance, secret information. It feels at times like there are even traitors among our own people. If we did not have such a tight grip on our own genetic engineering, I would dare say a first tier traitor or two have hidden themselves in the inner council, if such a thing were possible. What does surprise me, however, is the level of sophistication the resistance displays. Their ability to communicate between worlds is troubling. But if you could discover even some of the underlings in this conspiracy, it could lead us to the masterminds. And I guarantee that if you do find for us members of the resistance here on our home planet, you will be richly rewarded by the Council, and so too will your people."

Taliah suddenly sensed the hypnotic pool of Arum-Ton. Without warning, his mind began to gently probe hers. It was an oddly pleasant, disarming sensation, and she fought it the only way she knew how, by slipping into an alternate Taliah. An actor Taliah. A girl who was as faithful to the Overlords as a husband is to a beloved wife. She hoped she could maintain her façade as Arum-Ton touched the shadows of her thoughts. Creating an alternate self was a strategy passed down to her by the higher up members of the resistance. Specifically, by those Overlords who secretly worked against their own people, as Arum-Ton and the others in the inner circle had as yet refused to consider a real possibility.

"You are a good and faithful girl," said Arum-Ton. "I trust you with this knowledge of my own race's dilemma. Please come back and visit me if you find anything. I am hopeful for your people."

Arum-Ton nodded in a way that Taliah knew was a signal that she should now depart. Overstay her welcome, and all the goodwill she had built these many years would be gone in an instant.

Taliah stood erect. "Thank you for your trust in me, Arum-Ton. I will not disappoint you."

She bowed and then turned and entered the pod waiting for her. As it returned to the mother chamber she held herself together, reigning in her emotions. In the Palisade she wasn't sure it was safe. It wasn't until she reached the long winding path toward the arena cells where the fighters stayed did she finally let down her guard and began to cry.

The thought of her people being freed moved her deeply. But she could never free them at the cost of betraying the other worlds that were fighting so bravely against their Overlord masters. Arum-Ton trusted her. Her ability to evade his telepathic probing sparked a thought in her. With his confidence in her so high, might that enable her to do something crippling to the Overlords? Might she be able to use this relationship to her advantage?

Her thoughts dwelt on this as she walked the long road that led to her arena team.

* * *

Carter looked up as Taliah entered the cell. Nikolai lay on his bed having returned only an hour before from the medical rooms. He slept, recovering from his near fatal hit. When he saw him land as hard as he did when their opponent's shot hit his anti-grav unit, Carter thought he was dead for sure. He feared the cloud of dust that rose above him after he slammed into the arena floor would be his burial covering. But Nikolai had somehow survived the impact, and was brought to the medtechs in time.

Han sat cross-legged on his bed staring at his hands. What he was thinking about the last hour as he sat like a statue head down, Carter could only guess. As for Carter himself, his arm hurt only faintly now. The medical abilities of the Overlords amazed him. The damage from the gaping wound was now only a scar, the inner tissue healing a hundred times faster than it would have on its own.

"You are all alive," Taliah declared with a little more emotion than usual. "I am proud of you and I want to congratulate you."

Han's statue-like gaze lifted from his hands to peer up at Taliah. "Where is the honor of killing people we do not know from worlds that may very well be the same as our own people? People who are good, and noble, and worthy. My conscience isn't so clean."

"That isn't a good path to let you mind wander down," Taliah replied. "But remember this: You know your own world, the good and the bad, so fight for them. Do not surrender to a world you do not know. That would be risking all the good people back home."

Han sat silent again, his gaze falling back down to his hands.

Carter thought of Clarence, the man who he could not kill. The man who broke him from his murderous ways. He had defied human logic; losing his fear of death, seemingly to have his hope placed on the certainty that this life was not the end. That one's last breath escaping their lips would be met with what was next to come on the other side of death. This was what Carter had been thinking about ever since he'd returned to his cell, his wound healing, his fear of death fading. But there was still fear. Fear for his world, and the billions of lives that had no idea they were being placed in the hands of three men fighting for them on an alien planet. And Han's observation that their opponents were in the same position as they were, fighting for the good people back home. And yet, what was so ironic was that the Overlords seemed to choose the darkest man, and those most adept at killing—the murderers and the rogues—to save their world.

"How are you feeling Carter?" asked Taliah.

"Like Han, but as you said, I can only fight for what I know, and I know there are billions of people back home that need me to win."

Nikolai turned with a groan in his bed, but seemed to still be asleep.

Taliah came alongside Carter and gently touched his wounded arm, then withdrew her hand. "You have two more matches. There are only four teams left."

"Who is our next opponent?" asked Han. His question sounded like it had a purpose behind it. She studied his face. Whatever thoughts lay behind it, it appeared she couldn't read them. "And how many of them are there?"

"One man. Only one. But he is a very dangerous man."

The worry lines on Nikolai's forehead softened. "But with three of us," he said, "we should easily overwhelm him."

"You would think so," Taliah replied. "But he's been a one-man team since the very beginning. In their first match, his three teammates died, but he easily overcame his opponents. In his subsequent two matches, he has single-handedly killed a team of two, followed by a team of three. I would say he's every bit as dangerous as a four-man team."

"How long until our next match?" Han asked in the same efficient tone as before.

"Two days. It will be held at midday."

"I fight well in the heat," Han declared. For some, the way he spoke might come off as bravado or bragging. Not him, thought Carter. It wasn't Han's way. Yes, he derived confidence from his abilities, but a strong streak of humility existed there too. He was a man of truth who shared honestly what he thought and felt, and nothing more. "What kind of weapons will we be using?"

She paused before answering. "You will be given no weapons in this arena."

"That suits me just fine," said Han. "What do you think, Carter?"

Carter gave a long look at Han then turned his eyes to Taliah. "Killing is killing, but, to kill someone with a gun is far easier than looking at them up close, seeing the fear there. Watching their life slip away. It's a horrible thing to witness. Something I always tried to avoid when I was a hitman. I call them ghosts. The ones who looked me in the eyes as their life left them. Those ghosts still haunt me. They will never leave my memory."

Taliah's hand found Carter's shoulder again, and gently

stroked his back.

"I am surprised," said Han. "For a trainer of killers, you seem unusually compassionate at times. Though you drive us hard in training, there is another side to you, one that does not befit warfare."

Taliah removed her hand. "Sometimes I can't help but take off my mask. I am good at training fighters. I have no say who the Overlords choose. If they choose killers and murderers and the most grotesque men and women from other worlds to battle in the arena, then I work with whoever they give me. I guess it makes it easier that way. If I trained the common people from these worlds, I could never bring myself to send them out to kill."

Taliah looked at Carter, then quickly turned away.

"I must go now," she said, choking down the emotion in her words. "Rest, recuperate. Tomorrow we will begin the training afresh."

CHAPTER 12

"Our trainer is unstable," said Han. "I see the conflict in her eyes and in the way she expresses her feelings towards you."

His comment came out of the blue for Carter. "Feelings?" he asked. "What feelings?"

"I know how women behave in my homeland. And it is the same all across Earth. But what I've come to discover on this planet is that male and female traits extend across the universe. Taliah clearly has feelings for you. I see it in her movements, in the way she continually glances at you to watch your reactions to what is being said."

Carter frowned. "You're crazy. I've always frightened women. I've been told that by the men I worked for who knows how many times. They said I had the look of a killer. It explained why their wives and girlfriends never cared to be around me. And when I went out on occasion to a bar after completing a contract, I'd sit there and drink and drink, but never once did a woman approach me. Not that I ever cared. I went there to forget my life."

"You don't strike me as having the look of a killer. You must have lost it. I heard your story. Back on Earth I'd say your change of heart would be a good thing to most people. But here on this planet, well, you've managed to fight well so far, and somewhere along the way you've also managed to tug on the heartstrings of our trainer." Han's gaze drifted toward the stars above. "I do not see it as a bad thing though. It will make her prepare us all the more vigorously for the next match if her heart is turned towards you. If she doesn't want you to die, you can be sure she'll train us with everything she has."

Carter looked at Han and narrowed his eyes. "You're seriously convinced she's attracted to me?"

"I assume so," said Han, raising an eyebrow. "At the very least, she has affection for you."

Carter smiled. "What about you, Han? You can fight and you know how to kill, but you don't strike me as a killer, not of the kind I used to be."

A sliver of silence slipped into the cell. In the background, several plinks of water dripped onto the ground before Han moved. His shoulders rose with a deep breath before he turned around. He exhaled.

"I too have traveled a dark road for a time. In my youth I killed many men I shouldn't have. It may as well be called murder. I was consumed with my skills, and had an ego every bit as large as my abilities." Han brought up his hands and studied them. "I fought in underground martial arts tournaments. Fights to the death. There was a great deal of money bet between each fight, and I made a small fortune. But once my youthful pride faded, I learned honor and wisdom from a master teacher. I suppose the Overlords miscalculated when they arranged their team from Earth. Too many killers with hearts. Of course, you, Carter, may have surprised them there. They probably didn't know about your deconversion from being a hired assassin."

"No, I surprised even myself with that."

Carter lay back down on his bunk and closed his eyes. He was tired of the thought of another arena battle looming a few days from now, and it pressed down upon him. So did Han's words about Taliah, but in a different way. Had he changed so much that his face took on the look of a different kind of man? He had not seen himself in a mirror for a long time; what would he find there if he did? Would it be the same man he remembered?

* * *

Taliah sat on a black volcanic rock hidden away from the site of the sniffer drone overhead. The large green fronds seemed to trap the heat, but at least they kept out their eyes. Always probing. Always looking for anyone breaking the rules.

The jungle was sweltering today, and her face, arms, and clothing felt drenched by the humid air. She was taking an enormous risk meeting Telmar and Regin again, but the resistance movement was on the verge of exploding. The situation called for desperate action. If they had a chance at all it was worth taking, it was worth risking. She'd give her life to free the many worlds who'd suffered as hers did under the Overlords' despotic rule. She was willing to pay any price if the result was their downfall.

Ahead of her, a large green frond shook, and then a leaf the size of a man swept aside and Telmar and Regin's faces appeared out of the undergrowth.

"There you are," said Regin.

Another person appeared behind them—not a person, but an Overlord.

Her instinct to fight kicked in without a moment's thought. She crouched down into an attack position, her hands like steel hammers. Every muscle in her body ready to spring, they relaxed when Taliah recognized who had come with them.

Zoar-Wrel.

What was she doing here?! Far too much was being risked having her here! Zoar-Wrel was one of three Overlords who had joined the resistance. She was an enigma—a miscalculation. Like the other two Overlords born with too much sympathy, Zoar-Wrel had been unable to support the continued cruelty inflicted upon the enslaved worlds. She felt sorrow and pain at what her people were doing. Despite the yearly updates to her mind, her heart had been set on freeing the oppressed peoples being crushed by her own.

Though only a third level tier, Zoar-Wrel was the most crucial of the Overlords to support their cause for one simple reason. She worked at the Positron Core Center. A combination of subjugation and terror had been effective tools that helped maintain their control over other civilizations, but it didn't mean anything without power. Not the power of the inner council, and those that served under them, but the power that made space travel possible. That was the purpose the center served. The energy source the positron generators created meant every ship in the fleet had the power needed for not only faster than light travel, but also for the massive weapons that had the ability to destroy entire worlds, channeled to them from a single source.

Zoar-Wrel attempted to smile, though her half-humanoid, half-reptilian face had not been designed for that particular skill.

"What are you doing here?" Taliah groused, unable to hide the anger in her voice. "You let us slaves risk our lives with these meetings, but not you. You are far too precious to lose."

"I'm afraid the stakes are too high," said Zoar-Wrel. "My

people are closing in on the transmitter. Once it's found, they will know there are traitors among them. We have to act soon. Once they capture the transmitter we lose all communication between the slave worlds, and that means there is no possibility for a coordinated attack."

She was right. The transmitter was the key aid to the rebellion. Zoar-Wrel had secretly programmed it herself, a code that fed off the same positron energy her people used to keep the worlds in check. If the device were ever discovered, there would be no question amongst the Overlords that they had miscalculated the genetic control over their offspring, and that there were those amongst themselves working for the resistance. It didn't take a person of great intelligence to realize their response would be swift and thorough. Then all hope would be lost.

"How much time do we have?" asked Taliah.

"A matter of days," Zoar-Wrel replied. "They already know communication is happening between the slave worlds. They just haven't figured out how. But they are scanning every piece of code in the entire positron network and my embedded signal can't stay hidden forever, no matter how deeply I've buried it. Everything is in place to shut down the positron system, but we need one of your arena fighters to accomplish the final step that will bring down the system."

Zoar-Wrel had had the plan laid out for two years now. Taliah knew this day would come sooner or later, which meant the urgency to keep her team alive became more important than ever. She felt the weight of it on her shoulders. The hundreds of worlds enslaved all needed her skill. But their collective fate was not completely in her hands. Not at all. Her team had to survive the next round, then there would be the final match. Every Overlord on Arena Planet would be watching that match. It was the perfect opportunity for the rebellion to start, but as the plan stood she needed one of her team members to do something nearly unthinkable—something she could hardly imagine doing herself if she had been asked.

Zoar-Wrel handed Taliah a small capsule. "Whichever team member you choose, they must swallow this. It's time-sequenced and programmed. Just as we discussed." The third tier Overlord looked down at her with compassion.

"You've seen how they fought in the arena," said Taliah. "Only one loss in three matches. I believe Carter has been the primary reason for that. I don't have to tell you how he carried out his objective despite a terrible injury suffered against a worthy opponent. Most impressive, wouldn't you say?"

Telmar spoke up. "Do you think he will help us? His role is as crucial as anyone here."

"If he will help, I cannot say. But he is a good man. All we can do is have faith."

"Your team's next match is three versus one. Those are good odds."

"Normally, yes, but don't forget who they'll be fighting," Taliah continued. "Menseratis of the Kohlani System."

Telmar's expression turned dour. He gave a nod.

Regin said, "All we can do is move forward with our plans and be hopeful."

"I'll contact you again when everything has been set," said Taliah. She looked over her shoulder before she turned and faced the three before her. There was more she wanted to say. Needed to say. But it served no purpose, other than to risk being discovered by the sniffer drones. If they were caught, then their subversive movement would be squashed without mercy. "Stay safe."

Taliah disappeared in the tall growth, fearful they would be found out before the revolution had begun.

CHAPTER 13

Carter felt something gently touch his arm. Taliah's face appeared before him. A broad smile parted her full lips, though the setting behind her felt strange. Not different. Not otherworldly. But familiar. Very familiar.

As he looked about, the truth of where he found himself overwhelmed his senses. It was an Earthly setting. Waves crashed in the background, and Taliah looked almost like any other human on Earth. Carter basked in her touch, a tingling that was more than just a pleasant feeling. Something deeper at the core of him warmed at her touch.

He felt the hand on his shoulder brush more insistently, and suddenly Carter opened his eyes. In the dim lit cell, hovering above his bunk was a face. But it was not Taliah's. It was the strange reptile-like creature of an Overlord, similar in appearance as the ones he'd seen in the medical rooms after their last match. Or he might have assumed the lizard creature to be one of the oppressors who watched others die for their own amusement. Perhaps they too had been enslaved by the Overlords, forced to heal each combatant to better ensure a more enjoyable match. Whatever their status, he couldn't deny the doctors' medical skills were nothing short of miraculous.

"You need to follow me," the creature said in an authoritative tone. "Your arm needs additional attention. My fellow Overlords will not take it well if we are delayed."

Still groggy, Carter sat up. He had his answer. The Overlord's face remained expressionless, or at least, Carter did not know how to read it. Behind him was another holding one of the pain inflicting sticks.

Carter nodded and stood. The medical Overlord led him out of the room and the guard followed close behind, tapping his stick against his clawed hands.

He didn't understand why he needed to return to the medical rooms. His arm felt almost completely healed. But he didn't dare question anything, especially with the stick-wielding guard behind him.

The medical rooms were located on the far end of the arena. Outside the prison, a vehicle waited. The craft hovered above the ground nearly silent, only a faint pulse of some kind of electrical charge hummed in the air. The ride to the medical rooms was quick and they exited the vehicle. Carter found himself led down a long corridor lined with doors, finally stopping at one that looked like any other.

The medical officer turned and bowed to the guard. "Thank you, Tor-Kel. Tap once on the door if there is cause for alarm. We must be extra careful."

"Of course," said the guard.

What did that mean, Carter pondered? Who could they possibly be watching out for? The door swung open and Carter entered the room. To his surprise he saw Taliah seated beside the metal examination table.

"Why am I here?" Carter asked. "My arm feels like it's almost back to normal."

"Sit down," said the Overlord, who turned to Taliah. "I will give you some privacy now. Tor-Kel will tap once on the door if someone is coming."

"Thank you, Ywen-On," said Taliah, then she turned to Carter as the medical officer left through the door they had just entered.

"What's going on?" said Carter, more as an accusation than a question. "Why are those two Overlords behaving like you're their friend?"

Hesitancy crossed her face, which he didn't take as a good sign. "Carter, I have a difficult favor to ask you. It's more than a favor. Ywen-On, a medical officer, and Tor-Kel, the guard outside the door, they do not follow their people's ways." She looked around as if searching through thousands of different things to say, and just as important, where to begin. "There is a resistance movement here on the Arena Planet, and it reaches to the hundreds of worlds enslaved by the Overlords. Ywen-On and Tor-Kel are a part of it, and there is one other with us. Three in all."

Carter searched her eyes and saw the fear in them. Whatever she was about to ask him, she was putting a lot on the line. But he saw more than that in her eyes—beautiful and exotic and strange as they held fixed on his own—he also saw desperation and urgency. Never a good combination.

"Before you ask me your favor, I want to know how this rebellion you're referring to will affect Earth, my home world."

Taliah drew in a breath before answering. The action seemed to give her the courage she needed. "If everything goes according to plan, not only your planet and those your team has conquered in the arena will be saved, but also the hundreds of others currently enslaved. Each world would have a fair chance to overthrow the Overlord troops that keep them in subjugation. Currently, they have an energy power that gives them an unquestioned advantage. It's the Positron Core Center located in a well-guarded facility not far from where the arenas are located. We can disrupt this energy source that fuels the Overlord's entire fleet, including weapons such as the prodding sticks you yourself have felt. All of these would lose their power, rendering the Overlords weaponless."

It all sounded so good. Easy. Just one problem, nothing came that easy. Not with a race that conquered countless civilizations across the galaxy.

"There's something you're not telling me."

A short nod preceded her answer. "Observant, and correct." She forced a smile, but it quickly faded. "I must be honest. There is a downside for you."

"Which would be?" asked Carter.

"If you help us, you forfeit the opportunity to win the games, and that means your only chance of survival, or your world's survival, is defeating the Overlords by doing exactly what I am about to ask you to do."

"If my team wins," said Carter, "then Earth will not be enslaved, but at what cost?"

Taliah fixed her gaze on him. "You mentioned God to me earlier. It seems to me your arrival at this time on Arena Planet is not a coincidence, but a destiny. It is not often the Overlords make a mistake in choosing a kind soul to fight in the games. You are just the right person at just the right time."

"What is it you want me to do?" said Carter, his impatience

growing.

Taliah leaned close to him, her hand sliding over his own. Her eyes turned glassy, as if she were about to cry. He wondered if people from her world actually could. "I need you to die in the next round of fighting."

The words hung in the air incomprehensible. They were as clear as crystal, and yet, beyond reason. "Why?"

"I need you to die so that your existence will be erased from Arena Planet." She took her hand from his and crossed her arms tight. "Before you get too angry, let me explain what that means and why it is so crucial."

"I should hope so."

His unexpected outburst rattled her a second, but she quickly recovered. "You have in your brain a device placed there by the Overlords that tracks your every movement, identifies you when-ever you cross a security threshold. We need this to be re-moved."

"What good is that if I'm dead?"

Taliah reached out and squeezed his hand, then smiled thinly. "If all goes well and our plan is not disrupted, you will be brought back to life. The Overlords have the means to resurrect a dead person, but only if they have not been dead too long. For when the body begins to die, the cells become unrepairable after a time. When this exact moment is, we do not know. A day. Maybe two."

"So you want me to die so that the Overlords will remove tracking devices out of my brain, and then you plan to bring me back to life—to do what?"

"To infiltrate the Positron energy facility and destroy the source of the Overlords' power. The Harcovian Crystals. It has

taken six thousand years to grow them the size they are now."
Taliah held up her hand and opened her thumb and forefinger
as wide as it could go. "That small crystal is all that's needed for
the Overlords to bring about the massive evil they have wrought
across so many unsuspecting worlds. If we can stop them now,
how many countless others will be spared the enslavement or
destruction that too many have already tasted?" She paused a
moment. "Neutralize the crystals, and the Raxion Union is finished."

Tears ran down Taliah's face. Were they ones of joy or sadness, he wondered? But he also couldn't deny they were not so
different after all. Carter felt his chest churning at the immensity
of what she had asked him to do, but also what it would mean
for so many people beyond his own world if he trusted her and
this resistance movement he knew nothing of. Nothing beyond
this alien female's words.

Carter met Taliah's eyes and found himself deeply pulled
into the very heart of her. There was so much pain and fear
clashing fiercely behind her eyes, fighting against the hope of
what was possible. The freedom of the people she cared about,
both on her home world, and all the others he would never
know.

He raised his hand and wiped at the line of tears on her face.
The answer seemed simple. Of course he should try to save billions of lives under the boot of a brutal oppressor, and prevent
the future terror of billions more. Of course he should if he had
any sense of what was right and wrong. How could he be so self-
ish as to try and win the game if only for his own world's sake?
So that Earth would only be ruled by the Overlords, but not enslaved. What kind of simple choice was this, and yet, to ask a

man to die...

It was an incredibly horrifying prospect, to purposely set out to die.

And then another horrible realization dawned upon him. In the next arena, there were no weapons. What kind of death did that entail? Likely not a quick one.

Carter found Taliah's eyes once again and noticed the pain in them had changed. In them he now saw her pain for him. What she had asked him to do weighed heavily upon her as she had watched him contemplate such a horrific request.

What could he do but accept? What could he do but embrace his fate and follow what was right?

"I will," he said. "I'll do as you have asked."

Taliah suddenly cupped his head in her hands as fresh tears ran down both cheeks. She leaned her forehead against his. "Thank you," she said. "Thank you."

CHAPTER 14

Telmin-Kai sat back in his chair and looked up at the thousands of flickers of light in the auburn sky, far more than he normally saw. Just two times a year, on the first day of the fifth and fourteenth months, the orbits of all three moons swung them around to the opposite side of the planet during the nighttime hours, their luminescent disks positioned below the eastern horizon. On those rare astronomical occurrences he lost himself in the evening twilight whenever the opportunity presented itself. Him and most of the other Overlords he knew. Though for them, it was a chance to bask in the greatness of their empire. Without exception, every star that flickered in the sky hosted a solar system that had been conquered several generations back. For him, it was always gratifying to see the extent of their control over the galaxy.

"Glorious," he said to himself.

He took a sip of Tarkanian bitter water, the cup in his hand feeling colder than usual. The tepid air put out by the atmosphere machines kept the Arena Planet a steady three hundred millidegrees at any given time. Telmin-Kai relished those opportunities when a timely refreshment brought a measure of relief from the heat. Not that he minded it much. It would never go

over well if he complained about something as mundane as the
weather in front of his fellow Overlords. Self-discipline and ad-
herence to duty were all that mattered. It was what made them
strong. No weaknesses revealed in the face of one's enemies or
any thought of surrender. Only conquer and dominate lesser
worlds. That was the true purpose the arena matches served.
Learning a new technique of fighting or strategy was certainly a
benefit, but one side pitted against the other, the stronger of the
two surviving to fight another day. The thought of pure combat
against an alien opponent almost made him feel giddy.

Telmin-Kai wondered what it would be like if he fought in
the arena. With two days left before the next scheduled matches,
the idea intrigued him. But it would never happen. He had the
duty of observing both sides as they fought against each other,
gleaning whatever fighting techniques that impressed him, not
engage an inferior species to a few rounds of combat for his own
enjoyment.

Still, he thought, it would be an interesting experience.

A lone bodyguard held his position on the far side of the observer deck. He had been so still, Telmin-Kai forgot he was
there. It felt strange not having a member of the inner council
with him, such as that toad that followed Sulit-Bay everywhere he
went, engaged in the latest court politics, or assessing the loyalty
of a lesser government official. He found such matters tiresome,
and avoided those topics whenever possible. What he wished for
was a command of his own. Out there, on the fringes of known
space on a retribution ship, where his word was law, that and a
hundred new worlds to conquer, all within reach of his nimble
grasp.

Telmin-Kai sighed heavily. Five times he had requested a

reassignment into the Fremin quadrant, and five times his request had been denied by the High Magistrate Raxon-Pal. Deemed a vital necessity here, the rest of his life would be spent on the Arena Planet, writing his reports, and submitting them to his superiors for the benefit of the Empire. But what about the Empire's duty to him? It would take an event of supernova proportions to break the planet's lock on his life.

A pair of heavy boots clomped against the deck. Telmin-Kai's bodyguard reached for his weapon, but released his grasp on it when he recognized Sulit-Bay.

"Leave us," the first tier ordered him.

Telmin-Kai recognized that tone. His superior was in a foul mood, and there was no one to take it out on but him. Served him right for watching the stars on the observer deck rather than in his own quarters, like the other Overlords.

"This is a surprise," Telmin-Kai said. He figured it might go better for him if he took the initiative.

"I'm not here for idle talk. There is an important matter that merits discussion."

Perhaps the situation was worse than Telmin-Kai suspected. With few exceptions, the first tier usually enjoyed a short period of banalities before getting to the matter at hand. It helped him focus his thoughts, he often said. But when he launched straight into business, that meant there had been an important development, and not usually a good one.

With the two of them alone, Telmin-Kai knew he could speak freely, so long as he showed his superior the proper respect.

"Whatever it is, you know you can count on my discretion."

"That is why I sought you out."

Telmin-Kai waited. As he did, a thousand different scenarios fluttered through his mind. Had there been a coup? An uprising on some far off planet? Perhaps something closer to home, like a lesser official who made a grievous mistake that cost the first tier in some way. Whatever it was, he knew he'd find out when the Sulit-Bey was ready. Fortunately for him, he didn't have to wait long.

"I'm sure you've heard the rumors of a group of malcontents that is plotting the overthrow of the Raxion Union."

From his first day as a fourth tier Overlord he had heard of such rumblings. The years came and went, but none of them ever materialized. Just talk. "Of course. Nothing new about that."

"One of the problems of enjoying absolute control over one's enemies is the tendency to grow complacent. Too comfortable in your own unassailable position. Trust me when I say no position in the Empire is truly safe. Enemies lurk behind every dark corner."

Telmin-Kai didn't know where the first tier was going with this, but it unnerved him. Then an even more disturbing thought pressed into the forefront of his mind. Could Sulit-Bay be talking about him? "As I said before, you can count on my discretion." He placed his hand on the first tier's shoulder and let it linger there for effect.

His superior turned both ways, just to make certain they were alone. "I have had certain individuals under surveillance for some time. People of importance within their sphere of influence. Their movements have been monitored, those they associate with carefully noted. It took some time before I discovered anything of importance, but I believe a conspiracy bigger than we have ever encountered before is on the verge of instigating an open revolt against the Empire. Not one world or two, but dozens, if not hundreds."

Telmin-Kai pulled his hand back and he pondered the words. Specifically—revolt. Was such a thing possible?

"You must be mistaken. Sniffer drones patrol each world, transmissions are regularly monitored. The first hint of rebellion, and our shock troops would crush it in an instant."

Sulit-Bay went to the nearest view screen and studied the image. Tall trees with luminescent plumage swayed back and forth in a stiff wind. Below them, steep mountains rose above a sandy plain. The sight of the next arena match. "Our enemies are smarter than we give them credit for. A subtle nod from one passerby to another, instructions written on microscopic texts, clandestine meetings in plazas filled with people. Discontentment can breed many such covert acts of defiance. And the longer it is permitted, the more brazen they become."

"But I haven't heard even a whiff of what you have suggested."

"That is the point, and their goal. The closer you are to danger, the less obvious it is."

The last part of what Sulit-Bay said struck a nerve in him. It wasn't an idle threat or a random accusation. There was a point to it, and Telmin-Kai feared where it would stick.

"Does anyone else know of your suspicions?"

The first tier shook his head. "Only you. The trouble with conspiracies is that you don't know how high they go, or how broad."

If his superior had been as thorough in his investigation as he suggested, then there was only one way he'd feel safe divulging it to him. "You had me followed, didn't you?"

Sulit-Bay didn't shrink back at the accusation, which let the second tier know he was right. "A necessary precaution. I need to know who my allies are just as much as my enemies." He corrected himself. "Our enemies."

"I should be angry with you for what you did." Telmin-Kai paused a moment. "I could go to the inner council and discuss your, how shall we say... aggressive posture. But based on what you have discovered, I can understand your reasons." The only problem for Telmin-Kai, he still didn't know what the first tier had discovered, other than an unspecified fear of revolt.

"One week ago, you talked of your admiration for Taliah of Axinar IV."

"Yes."

Sulit-Bay peered close at him. "How well do you know her?"

"As well as any other trainer. No more or no less than one from another. It's her fighting skills I respect, not the person."

"I fear she's put those fighting skills to use in ways that could prove dangerous."

Again, a general threat without substance. His vague notions of danger were beginning to grow tiresome. "You've said a threat exists that has the potential to undermine the Raxion Union. But so far, there's not been one shred of proof to substantiate your claim. It's late and I'm tired. If you can't give me one piece of solid evidence, then I bid you goodnight."

Telmin-Kai turned for the door, but was stopped by the first tier. "It may surprise you to know meetings in the lower caves have been held by Taliah and other people from her home world."

"That doesn't sound so menacing."

"If an Overlord were present, would you consider that normal?"

No, he must have heard him wrong. One of their own, meeting in a part of the arena complex that has been designated off limits? It wasn't possible.

"And this same trainer who may have recruited an arena fighter with a growing reputation."

Only one person he knew who fit that description. "Carter Stone."

"The one and the same."

"I... I don't understand how it all fits together."

"You will soon enough."

Sulit-Bay clapped his hands together.

From the far end of the observer deck, two guards dragged in a man who didn't move. Blue blood covered his torn clothes and swollen face. They threw him onto the deck and took a step back.

Telmin-Kai thought the interrogators had done their job too well. What was left of the man face down on the deck looked on the verge of death. He lay still a moment before his fingers twitched, followed by a labored breath.

"Who is this?" Telmin-Kai demanded.

One of the guards reached down and grabbed the man's head, snapping it upward.

The unnamed prisoner winced in pain.

"Identify yourself," Sulit-Bay ordered.

A pained breath burst from his lungs. He tried to rise, but lacked the strength. The second guard came alongside the first and they jerked him to his feet.

"Your name," Sulit-Bay repeated. His voice had softened, as though bidding a friend to answer.

"I..." the beaten man stammered. His head fell forward and hung there until the first guard wrenched it up again. "My name is... Regin... of Axinar IV."

CHAPTER 15

The air felt heavy that night. And the heat. Had it grown hotter since they first arrived on this wretched planet? It felt that way to Carter. He lay back on his mat and stared at the rocky ceiling above. In the background, the same monotonous plinking of water sounded in his ears.

Feeling restless, he sat up and gazed at the stars. Carter couldn't put his finger on why, but they appeared brighter than normal, and more numerous. Or his eyes had adjusted to the dark in a way they hadn't on previous nights.

"No moons," Nikolai said.

"What?" Carter asked.

"Have you noticed there are only stars in the sky tonight? Not a single moon to be seen, crescent or otherwise. First time that's happened since we were brought here."

"Not brought," Carter corrected him. "Abducted against our will. I wish I'd never heard of this place."

He turned in Han's direction, who appeared to be sound asleep. He lay flat on his back, his hands clasped together over his stomach, rhythmic rising and lowering of his chest the sole indicator of just how deep he slept.

"I envy him sometimes," Carter commented, his tone wistful.

"After a long day of training, the moment we step into this cage, he flips a switch in his head and acts like he's camping with friends or something. I can't turn it off like that."

Nikolai got to his feet. A small moan of pain slipped past his lips as he straightened. "I'm not surprised he blinked out the moment he closed his eyes. Taliah pushed us pretty hard today. Tomorrow will be no better. Reminds me of my days as a sub-mariner."

"I'm guessing you have a tale or two to tell."

"Not as much as you'd think. Mostly, it was the captain and his second in command drilling us for mock attacks, or making emergency dives, or running silent within sonar range or one of your fleets. You know, cat and mouse kinds of things." A grin of satisfaction appeared.

"Sounds exciting to me."

"It was, at first. But let me tell you, life on a submarine can get boring quick. You're underwater for weeks at a time. No sun. No fresh air. Just a metal casing around you twenty-four seven, and the stink. After a few days in that tin can, the whole of the submarine was pretty ripe. Most of the crew hoped something happened on board, anything that would break up the monotony."

"Such as being bombed by depth charges?"

"Nothing that dramatic. But a match between our side and yours, who would have won?"

Carter's gaze slipped downward. "Yes, the match," he said just above a whisper. Then he kicked at a rock, which banged off the wall nearest him, coming to a quick stop after it skittered across the stone floor.

"Wha... what's going on?" Han asked, startled awake. He

rubbed the sleep from his face.

Nikolai's eyebrows drew together. "What's gotten into you, Stone? You've been in a sour mood since you returned from the med center. Did they perform some alien experiments on you?"

Though the Russian didn't intend for his question to sound humorous, it came off that way in Carter's head. A weak smile formed before it straightened out again. "No. Nothing like that."

"Then what's your problem?"

Han, obviously annoyed at being awakened in the abrupt manner, inched up with his elbows. "Can't this wait until morning? We've a long day ahead of us, and I'm exhausted."

Though his question had been meant for them both, Carter couldn't shake the feeling it was directed more at him than the Russian.

"You haven't answered my question," Nikolai persisted like a dog who had sunk his teeth into his favorite bone. "Something's bugging you."

A quick eye-roll preceded Han lying back down on his mat. "Say whatever's on your mind, and then we can all get some sleep."

Whether intentional or not, Han's impatience gave Carter the impetus he needed to say what had been stuck in his thoughts since he had talked with Taliah. "I'm not going to survive the next match. I intend to sacrifice myself so that you two will live."

Nikolai spun around the same instant Han bolted up. "What?" they asked in unison.

Carter let the question hang in the air. He knew exactly what he said, but still couldn't believe he had agreed to Taliah's proposal.

"You're joking, right?" Nikolai chided him. The look on

Carter's face must have let him know this was no joke. His sunny
face turned into a scowl. "Why in the world would you do something like that? You getting planet happy?"

With a dismissive wave of his hand, Han shushed him.
"Please. You're only making this worse. Something's on Carter's
mind, and we won't get at the truth if you maintain an antagonistic attitude."

"No, it's okay," Carter said. He was glad he had finally gotten
it out in the open, part of the truth, anyway. It made what he
needed to say next a little easier. "I had planned on telling you
two in the morning, before we started training, but tonight will do
just as well. Better perhaps."

Several moments passed before Carter told them everything
Taliah had asked of him. When he got to the part about sacrific-
ing himself so the device in his head could be removed, Nikolai
balked at the idea of what he described as *going down without a
fight*. He argued the Overlords would know something was
wrong, and they might all be killed just on suspicion alone.

"No," Nikolai said as adamantly as he began. "It isn't right.
Stinks is a better way of putting it."

"Why do you object the way you do?" Han asked.

"An alien from halfway across the galaxy, who's only job is to
train us to kill others, tells you a story about slave worlds that
want to rebel against their masters, but can't until a savior comes
along and has to die in the arena so he can be smuggled into a
crystal chamber that powers their entire Empire. Am I the only
one that thinks this sounds a little crazy? What if she's lying?
What if she's setting us all up so we lose the next match?"

"Why would she do that? From what I've observed, she's just
as motivated to win each round as we are."

A hot breath pushed out of Nikolai. "You talk like you know her, you and your Zen ways, Chinese."

Han stormed over to Nikolai and grabbed him by the shirt. "I'm tired of your insults and derogatory comments." He shoved the Russian into the wall for emphasis. "Either you call me by my name, or you say nothing at all."

A disarming smile blossomed on Nikolai's face, which took some of the fight out of Han. His grip on Nikolai's shirt loosened.

As Han turned back toward his mat, Nikolai punched him in the kidney. Stunned a moment, Han swung his leg sideways, knocking the Russian to the ground. He then jumped on top of him and started hitting Nikolai in the face. Blood poured out of his nose after each blow.

"Stop it!" Carter yelled. He grabbed Han and pulled him off Nikolai. "This fighting is pointless."

Breathing heavily, Han wiped the blood off his hand with his shirt. "He's right. I don't know what got into me." He reached down and offered to help Nikolai up. "I'm sorry."

Nikolai spat on the ground. "You and me both." He slapped Han's hand away and slowly got to his feet. "You hit stronger than you look, Chinese."

"And you can take it better than I expected," Han said after a soft laugh.

Both men looked at one another in mutual admiration before they turned their attention back to Carter.

"My mind's made up," he said. "For the sake of the uprising, and Earth's future, I'm going to take the biggest gamble of my life and allow myself to be killed in the arena."

"You're right," Nikolai said. "It is a gamble, for you and for us. If you're wrong, then we just gave the other side a big advantage."

"What do you think, Han?" Carter asked. He wasn't sure if he wanted to hear the answer. If they both opposed his decision, then he might have to go back on his word. Which might not sit well with Taliah. How would she react if he did? Carter stopped himself. Why did he care what she thought?

"It means a dramatic shift in our fighting strategy. Since she's the one who broached this scheme of hers, then it has a better chance of success if we're all involved in its implementation."

Carter faced Nikolai, whose nose was still wet with blood. "I know how you feel about this, but if we have any chance of helping her people defeat the Overlords, and Earth in the process, it's all or nothing."

He let the question hang in the air. The longer it did, the more it felt like the cell walls pressed in on them.

Just when Carter was about to speak up, Nikolai shook his head. "I think you've been sent on a fool's errand, but I'm in."

"Now, can we finally get some sleep?" Han asked.

* * *

The metal clamps wrapped tight around Regin's wrists cut into his skin. The more he tried to loosen their hold on them, the more the sharpened edges did their work.

"You can try and escape but it won't do you any good."

Sulit-Bay stood over him, a look of satisfaction etched into his frozen expression. Beside him, though less confident, was Telmin-Kai.

The first tier nodded at a technician standing by a row of

lighted consoles. Several probes extended from one of them, all pointed at Regin's head. Even from across the room he felt their focused heat dig into his skull. Was this part of the torture, or did the two have something else in mind?

A tip of Sulit-Bay's head provided the answer. The technician waved his hand over the central console. It buzzed a moment, before the probes spun in a circular fashion. The faster they moved, the warmer it felt. Regin wanted to lift his hand and block the heat coming at him, but the clamps made that an impossibility.

A second, more subtle move of the technician's hand produced pain in Regin's body. It didn't hurt too much at first, but the longer the unpleasant sensation lasted the more discomfort he felt. It started in his chest, and spread through his extremities. It became sharper and more intense, until it felt like every part of him was on fire.

"Please," Regin cried out. "Make it stop."

Sulit-Bay bent closer, his face contorted into a twisted smile. "I will, when you tell me what Taliah's plans are."

His eyes closed tight, Regin fought against the pain growing in his body. "There are no plans. She is loyal to you."

"I wish I could believe you, but my surveillance of her suggests otherwise. Why did she meet with you and your brother, Telmar?"

"News... news f-f-from h-h-home." His eyes rolled back and everything went dark.

A slap to his face brought Regin back into consciousness again.

The clamps. The pain in his body. Then he remembered where he was. Deep in the bowels of the observer ship, locked away in a sound-proof room.

Telmin-Kai and Sulit-Bay conferred with one another in hushed whispers before the first tier turned in Regin's direction. He extended his hand toward the second tier. "My subordinate here feels this method of questioning will not produce satisfactory results. That in time, you will say anything to stop the pain. I disagree. I believe it can loosen the tightest tongue."

He pointed at the technician.

In an instant, a higher level of pain exploded in Regin's body, far more intensely than before.

"Tell me what I want to know. Which planets are planning to revolt against the Union?"

His jaw clenched tight, Regin forced the words out. "T-h-here is no, no, no revolt. Only... loyalty."

"You see," Telmin-Kai said, "your approach isn't working. He won't talk."

"I think he will."

The first tier motioned for the technician to switch off the device fitted with the probes. With a nod, the underling did as he was ordered, then turned and left the room a moment, returning with a translucent box that rested on his upturned hand. Amorphous shadows inside moved about in random directions.

Though they appeared harmless enough, Regin didn't have a good feeling about this. It wasn't within the Overlords' nature to give up so easily.

The technician gently handed the box to Sulit-Bay, who held it in front of Regin like an object of great value.

"Do you know what this is?" He asked him. "More specifically, what these are?"

Regin shook his head.

"Certainly, you've heard of bore worms before."

If Regin could jump out of his skin, he would. "No!" he cried out in terror. Known as the torturer's elegant scalpel, they dug into a person's flesh and burrowed deep inside until they came upon an exposed nerve. They'd attach themselves to it and consume one after the other, all the while inflicting a level of pain that drove most to insanity. But the bore worms never stopped until the person was dead. And once implanted into a person's body, they could not be removed. One way or another, he was going to die.

"Tell me what I want to know, and we can avoid all this unpleasantness." Sulit-Bay moved the box closer.

All his life Regin worried about one unpleasant thing after another that may befall him at any time. Until this moment, none of his fears had ever come true. An ironic thing, he thought. From nothing to experiencing the most excruciating death possible. If the worms were put on him, he'd tell the first tier everything he knew, all the while begging for his life to end. No. He didn't want to go out that way. Not for himself or his people. He and they deserved better.

"I'll tell you," Regin said, surrender tinting his voice, "Only..."

"Only what?"

"I cannot speak the information. It must be written down."

Telmin-Kai peered at him close, so close he felt his putrid breath brush against his face. "It appears he is telling the truth, strange as that sounds."

The box of bore worms remained in its place. "Are you certain?" Sulit Bay said. "We have been deceived by Axinarians before."

"It is how we in the resistance are conditioned. To keep from revealing secrets, our bodies experience a kind of paralysis when under duress. And no amount of force can unlock it. But we can write the information you require."

Sulit-Bay looked at him with suspicion. "What do you think?" he asked Telmin-Kai without facing him.

"What can it hurt? You unlock one hand, but he is still fastened to the chair. If he's lying, you still have use of the bore worms."

"A salient point."

Telmin-Kai nodded at the technician, who produced a magnetic key. The tech passed it over Regin's right hand, and the clamp retracted with a sharp clank.

Freed of the restraint, Regin lifted his arm, rivulets of dried blood covering it. He savored this short moment of freedom for as long as possible, knowing it would be the last he'd ever experience.

"Stylus and pad," the first tier ordered.

The same indifferent expression on his face, the technician turned for the consoles. When he did, Regin grabbed the hem of his cloak and produced a small white-capped needle. Before the Overlords could react, he plunged it into his leg.

A warm sensation swam through Regin's body. It felt like he was floating, the pain he experienced moments before a distant memory. His head rolled to one side, and the world around him blurred.

"What did you do?" Sulit-Bay asked through the fog.

"Rob you of your victory."

His pounding heart slowed as his perceptions of the room faded.

Blissful darkness.

* * *

Telmin-Kai put his hand on Regin's lifeless wrist. No pulse. He pulled it away in disgust.

"He's dead. Seems your threat with the bore worms had the opposite effect you intended."

"Mark your place," Sulit-Bay spat in reply, "or I will use them on you."

The second tier knew he had crossed a line in his accusation. He didn't suffer setbacks of this magnitude often, and he took it out on his superior. If they weren't such good friends, he'd be the one screaming out in pain. "Now that he's dead, what do you propose?"

Sulit-Bay pondered the question a moment. "Nothing more than an unanticipated delay. We know Taliah is involved. We concentrate our efforts on her."

CHAPTER 16

"His name is Menseratis, and he has natural regenerative capabilities."

"You're telling us the next fighter can heal himself?" Nikolai stared at Taliah like he didn't believe her.

"That's what I'm telling you," she replied.

"How fast does he recover?" questioned Han.

"Unless the wound is mortal, he will recuperate in a matter of minutes," said Taliah.

Carter watched Nikolai glare at their instructor while Han looked thoughtfully down at the floor. Taliah was still unaware that he had told Han and Nikolai about the secret plan. He guessed she would've preferred he hadn't said anything to his two teammates, but his conscience wouldn't allow him to keep it secret. They needed to know. Their lives were on the line once he died. And besides, if they knew, they could help Taliah.

Carter smiled. "So before I die, I better know Han and Nikolai are going to be able to kill this Superman enemy of ours."

Taliah frowned. A deep line cut down both sides of her face. She looked both angry and uncertain.

"I had to tell them. It wouldn't be right for them to lose me in battle without knowing ahead of time. That way, we can make it part of our strategy. My death, that is."

Taliah stared at Nikolai and Han. "You know?"

They both nodded.

"It's a stupid plan," Nikolai declared, "though I do see the benefits of it. If Carter can pull this off, you obviously have a strategy in mind for hurting the Overlords. I'm all for making it hurt for them."

Taliah looked pale. "Don't speak of this," she whispered. "Not here, not in the open. Speak of it only in code."

"Understood," said Nikolai.

"All right," said Han. "We have one more training session before our next match. We've got to get it right."

Taliah led them from the room into the small training arena. Carter was surprised to see that half of it had been transformed into a jungle, while the other half was a volcanic heap of rocks with what looked like the openings of caves dotting the mountainous rock pile.

"I assume this is what it's going to look like for our match," Carter concluded.

"Yes," Taliah answered him matter-of-factly. "This is a mini version of the arena you will be fighting.. Half of the enclosure is a sweltering hot jungle set at one hundred percent humidity. The other half is a cold barren volcanic spillway dotted with deep mines. This arena represents both of your worlds. Your enemy, Menseratis, lives on a jungle world, which I must warn you is far different than the jungles of your own home planet. The jungles on Fangsor 8 reach upwards of one hundred and thirty degrees in the shade, but on Menseratis' world he has no concept of the cold as you do. It will be tempting for him to remain on his side, just as it will be tempting for you to stay on yours."

"How cold is our side?" asked Han.

"To you it will not be very cold. On the surface, nearly sixty degrees. But in the mines, it may drop ten or twenty degrees. For Menseratis, this is unbearably cold."

"With one versus three, I imagine he's going to wait for us to come to him," Carter deduced. "To try and retain the element of surprise."

"What I want to know," said Nikolai as he stepped over to a large green frond and ripped it free, "is how we're going to find weapons. I don't see much to work with here."

"I see something I can work with," said Han. "That vegetation over there resembles bamboo, easily sharpened into a spear or knife."

"You will find this arena full of plants and rocks and other materials you can easily transform into weapons," said Taliah. "I suggest you spend some time exploring, seeing what kind of offensive and defensive strategies would work against Menseratis here in this arena."

"Us? You going somewhere?"

"I have some... business to attend to. Familiarize yourself with the plants and terrain, discover what you can use. I shall return not long from now."

* * *

"Regin's dead," whispered Telmar.

"What?" Taliah shook her head, not believing the news. "That's not possible." She had seen him just the day before, paranoid as usual with his neuroses. Always worried about what might happen. Telmar must be mistaken. "Are you sure?"

"Zoar-Wrel informed me a short while ago. That is why I summoned you."

The news hit her full force. Regin had been a friend and ally nearly the entire time she'd been on Arena Planet.

"Did he talk, or was he able to use his suicide vial in time?"

Telmar looked frightened, and he didn't frighten easy. "We don't know. There's no way to know."

"I'm so sorry this happened." She reached out and gave Telmar a heartfelt hug. He hugged her back, though with restraint. Did he not feel comfortable manifesting his emotions, she wondered?

"He wasn't the best of brothers, but I will miss him." His detached-self returned. "What do you think our next step should be?"

She pondered their options, few as they were. "We may not have an opportunity like this again in our lifetime. If he talked, it's over. If he didn't, then a hundred worlds hang in the balance. Until we hear otherwise, we have to assume he took the vial before he compromised the plan."

Stone-faced at first, Telmar's gaze fixed on her, as though sizing her up. "Yes. We have to assume as much. But something else is troubling me."

"What?"

"Why did they detain him in particular? Are we under surveillance? Do we have an operative in our midst? Either way, it's possible they have names. Perhaps they know of us."

Taliah nodded. "For the sake of those we wish to free, this must be our last communication. I sent a secret message to..." She looked around. "To the others. No more meeting together. We follow the plan from now on."

"So Carter is going to—"

"Quiet," shushed Taliah. "No more discussion. They could be listening. We follow the plan."

Telmar nodded. "Alright." He took Taliah's hand. "Be brave."

* * *

"Curses!" shouted Sulit-Bay. "That fool was about to tell us something."

"He mentioned Carter's name," said Telmin-Kai. "Carter knows something, or is going to do something."

"Yes, I heard."

"Do we take out Telmar and Taliah?" asked Telmin-Kai, "or do we bring them in and torture them?"

"No, not yet." We have a sniffer drone on them both. Chances are good we may find out much more by simply following the two traitors. But rest assured, we'll bring them in eventually."

"What about Carter?"

"Yes, we do need to do something to throw off their short-term plans. Whatever they want Carter to do, I'm going to make it very hard for him to do it."

"I don't know how. We can't eliminate him from the games. He's made quite the impression with the other Overlords."

"Watch and learn, Telmin-Kai. Watch and learn." Sulit-Bay's placid expression hardened. "We won't eliminate him. But there are other options that are just as effective."

* * *

Carter bent down next to Han, staring at the crude knife he had carved out of a bamboo stalk. Using a rock with a razor-thin edge, he shaved layer after layer of the rigid material, cutting it into a sharpened point. "This is how we do it. Spears. I am very good at throwing them. We make knives for close combat, and spears for long-range."

Nikolai came up beside them. "Come with me into the caves. I want to show you something."

His hurried demeanor didn't sit well with Carter. They still had a lot of work to do, and going off on some side trip of undetermined value only lessened the time they had for making weapons. And more importantly, practicing with them.

When Carter balked at his ill-timed distraction, Nikolai insisted. Han, for his part, didn't say anything. In fact, he hadn't said much since Carter first told him of his intentions for the next match.

As the two held their ground, Carter finally backed down. The quicker they got this over with, the sooner they'd finish the weapons.

Carter and Han followed Nikolai into one of the gaping cave mouths. The interior was pitch dark, especially after being in the bright sunlight all morning.

"You have to let your eyes adjust," Nikolai said. "We can't go all the way in, otherwise we may never come out. I don't know how deep these things go."

"What's so important that you dragged us up here?"

"Patience," Nikolai replied. "You'll see."

"If we can make a fire then we can explore the cave," Han suggested.

"Look here," said Nikolai. "Mining tools. An ax, a shovel.

These will definitely come in handy."

"The ax is cumbersome," said Han, "but perhaps you Russians prefer big, awkward weapons."

In the dim light, Carter could see a smile blossom on Nikolai's face.

Then something strange happened. Nikolai's demeanor darkened for a moment as something large went past the cave's mouth.

Nikolai's eyes hardened and Carter spun around.

A monstrous form stood just inside the rocky opening. All three men held their ground, frozen in shocked silence.

The huge form took a step forward. A rumbling noise issued from its throat.

"What's going on?" asked Nikolai. "I thought we were safe in the training arena?"

The creature began to move forward more swiftly. Nikolai picked up an ax and shouted, "Get back!"

The creature's pace only quickened.

"Go!" Shouted Carter, backpedaling.

"Where?" shouted Nikolai.

"Into the mine."

Nikolai threw the ax at the creature, but its large arm easily batted it away as if it were a twig.

Carter watched in terror as the creature grabbed Nikolai, but reacted with surprise when it tossed him aside, almost gently. In that moment Carter realized that this thing, whatever it was, was coming after him.

Carter turned and fled into the darkness, his hands feeling frantically along the rock wall, his only escape.

* * *

"I don't like this." Zoar-Wrel looked over her shoulder. Fear blazed in her slitted eyes, which did not go unnoticed by Telmar. "Taliah gave us our instructions. No contact with each other."

"I know that's the plan," he said, "but we must all be ready if we have any chance of success. The Raxion Union has informants everywhere."

A soft plink of water struck the tunnel floor. The two froze. When the perceived danger passed, they both turned again toward one another, the torch in Telmar's hand giving the barest of light. Anything more, and the nearest sniffer drone would pick up the heat signature.

Zoar-Wrel's pensive expression returned. Why was she this nervous, he wondered? If it weren't for her, there would be no planned revolt. Until she sought him out, he hadn't even considered the possibility of freedom for his people. Yes, he hated the Raxion Union with all his being, praying to his planet's host god to send them all into a black hole on the far side of the galaxy, but rebel against them, never. Yet, something had spooked her. Then a terrible thought entered Telmar's head. Was she having second thoughts?

"The death of my brother might give some of the planetary leaders aligned against the Union doubts about our chances of success. When you contact them at the pre-designated time with the final attack code, I must know they still support the insurrection before tomorrow's arena match. If just one backs out, it could put us all in very great danger."

"There are... concerns." Her words hung in the air a moment before she continued. "After I told you about what happened to

Regin, I informed the council, who then notified lower level magistrates. A number of them have voiced their fears of being exposed, and I can't blame them. Since yesterday, I too have wondered about the soundness of continuing with the plan, now that we know a breach of some kind exists. A delay might be prudent, until we can assess just how much Sulit-Bay has been told."

Telmar gave what she said a long thought. To her credit, she gave him the time he needed. A person ruled by their emotions would have persisted with their position, to the point of forcing a premature decision. Never a good thing. At least she had the sense to rein her fears and let the right choice be made.

"Just one more day. That's all we need. Carter Stone has agreed to let himself be killed in the arena so his implant can be removed, and then brought to the Positron Center. We might never get a chance like this again, even with the dangers involved."

This time, it was Zoar-Wrel who pondered his words. "Or the arena match can be the vehicle that exposes the insurrection before it is launched, and all of us rounded up and executed." She came within a hair's breadth of him and stared deeply into his eyes. "And what of yours and a hundred other home worlds? What happens to them if we fail?"

"I know the risks are great, but the thought of living under the shackles of the Raxion Union one more day is like a poison that is slowly killing me and my people."

"Now who's letting their emotions get the better of them?"

If only they knew what Sulit-Bay knew? Did his brother talk before he died? The thought of the bore worms used against him was almost too much for Telmar to bear. He hoped it hadn't come to that. But as terrible a thought of dying in terrible agony, a much worse one was the eradication of his home world by retribution ships if tomorrow's match was a trap.

He looked up and closed his eyes. "Creator of all, give me your wisdom. Should we proceed with the plan or call it off?" His breaths grew short and labored as he waited for an answer.

In the dark, though he couldn't see her directly, Telmar heard both of Zoar-Wrel's hearts pounding in synchronization. The steady beat, beat, beat had a calming effect on him. As he found himself drawn into its hypnotic effect, the confusion and uncertainty he experienced moments before subsided, replaced by clarity and conviction.

Telmar opened his eyes. "Tell the planetary leaders we proceed as planned."

CHAPTER 17

Deeper and deeper into the cave Carter fled. Somewhere ahead of him, the thrums of a great torrent echoed off the walls, as though a mighty river cut through the rock deep inside the cavern. Behind him, the scraping noises of what could only be the large pursuer's claws dragged and clicked against the rock flooring and walls.

Why was it here, Carter wanted to know? Was it because of Taliah? Was it because of his connection to the resistance? He feared it was. What was it going to do if it caught him?

Ahead, the rush of water grew louder, and the roar had now turned into a raucous crashing. Carter could no longer hear the creature behind him, but he knew it was still there. He felt panicked. With every step, he imagined it getting closer and closer. How many more steps did he have before the end came? Carter put his hands forward and blindly patted the rock wall ahead, towards the violent flow. What else could he do?

Carter got down on his hands and knees, sensing the underground river wasn't far off. The hard rock floor was wet, and he crawled forward until his hand slipped into the rushing water.

At that moment, something strong grabbed his calf and lifted his leg from the ground. Sharp pain erupted in the area where the creature's claws dug into his skin. Carter cried out, but the sound was lost in the roar of the river.

Carter kicked his leg with all his strength, and managed to break free from the creature's hold. Uncertain where it would take him, he lurched forward, diving hands outstretched into the water.

It was deep, and he could not feel the bottom as he was carried along by the torrent. In his panic, Carter imagined numerous rocky spikes hanging down from the ceiling, any one of which might strike him in the face, knocking him unconscious. He would surely drown if that happened. Doing his best to protect himself, Carter held out his hands, but the second he did he started to sink. Feet forward, he had no choice but tread water to the best of his ability as he hurtled down the river like a small leaf buffeted about without mercy.

He was certain the creature had not followed, until he heard a low growl very near him.

Desperation surged through his body. His strength all but gone, he somehow swam towards whatever shore the darkness hid at the edge of the river. But then reason told him to stop. He would be dashed against the rocks if he did.

The creature gnashed its sharpened teeth behind him. Perhaps five meters away, perhaps ten.

Suddenly, a soft light glowed ahead. Carter peered through the mist. Though he couldn't be sure, it appeared the river poured out of the rock mountain with great force. He braced himself. Growing closer by the second, the roar of the river turned into a crashing sound. At the lip of the cave he saw the water fall away. He clenched his fists tight and drew in a deep breath.

The next instant he plummeted over the side and tumbled down the sheer face for what felt like a thousand meters. All he could do was pray that the rocks below didn't dash him to pieces.

He didn't dare look. It wouldn't matter if he did. Suddenly, his body slammed into a pool of water, and in that moment he experienced immense relief despite the pain stinging his arms and legs from the impact. His body limp, it floated to the surface, and just in time. Just when it felt like his lungs were about to burst, his head broke through the surface, and he drew in the biggest breath of his life.

At that moment, a huge crash sounded over the thrum of the waterfall. Instinctively, Carter swam in the opposite direction. The water's edge came up on him quick as he paddled with all his strength to reach it. His hands clasped on a large bush growing over the bank and he used it to pull himself up. He was nearly out of the water, when he felt his leg again clasped in a grip so tight, he cried out in pain.

Rising out of the water was the creature. Only, now it hefted his body up into the air.

The thing was enormous. Then another thought struck Carter. It was not alive. Though the creature looked like an animal out of a nightmare, it was no animal. Rather, it was some kind of machine. It was the beast's eyes that gave it away. They glowed unnaturally, and panned back and forth in slow movements that were robotic in nature.

The mouth of the creature opened, and words that no animal tongue could speak came out in an eerie robotic tone. "We know you are working with Taliah. We know she is involved in a rebellion against the Overlords."

Had his head struck a rock, or did the creature just speak? "We could kill you here and now," said the robot creature. "Tell us what Taliah is doing. Tell us her plans, and you will live."

Carter stared at the hideous face a mere breath away. "I don't know what you're talking about. She hasn't told me anything. I am only a fighter contending for the survival of my planet. Those are the only plans I know about."

"That is possible," said the creature, "but unlikely. Just in case though..." The beast lifted one of its clawed hands, and on the tip of the longest finger was a mechanism that looked like a mechanical insect, only it had sharp needle-like things protruding from the head.

"Do you see it?" said the strange voice from the creature's mouth.

"Yes," Carter replied, still uncertain of the beast's intentions.

"This little device will allow me to kill you at any moment. I will be listening to every word you say, and if I detect you are working for Taliah and the resistance, this little bug I am placing inside you will kill you the moment I tell it to."

The creature's hand thrust forward as if it was going to strike the side of Carter's head.

Instead, he screamed as the insect was driven into his skull.

"If you cooperate, you will have the opportunity to save your world from enslavement. If you don't, then you will die."

* * *

Carter stumbled through the jungle. It was blindingly hot and he was desperately thirsty. In his time spent in the river, the last thing he thought of was to take a drink. But now, he wished he had. Driven by fatigue, he crawled on hands and knees toward the edge of the arena where the door stood open.

Nikolai spotted him and rushed over. "You're alive!" he said, then turned and shouted for Han.

"What happened to you?" continued Nikolai.

Carter shook his head; he had to be careful what he said. Taliah had told everyone to speak in code. He hoped Nikolai and Han remembered. If they slipped up, he knew the Overlords would be listening.

"I'm all right," said Carter. "Please, just give me some water."

Nikolai reached down for the container on his belt and gave Carter his drink.

"Did that thing catch you?"

Carter nodded. "It seemed to think I was part of some resistance." Carter sat up and tapped the side of his head with his finger. "I don't know what it was talking about. Have you heard anything about... some kind of resistance?" he said in an exaggerated manner.

Carter saw recognition dawn on Nikolai. "How strange," he said. "Perhaps it's a psychological element added to our next match."

"Perhaps," Carter repeated.

"I thought you were dead." Han said, concern tinting his voice.

"I thought I was too," said Carter. He turned toward Nikolai. "By the way, why did you bring us in the cave in the first place? What was so important that we needed to see?"

Nikolai's gaze dropped, as if embarrassed. "Oh, that. There were some crystals imbedded into the walls that looked like diamonds. Some big ones. I thought we could fashion them like arrowheads. You know, like the bows and arrows used by primitive men."

"I think Taliah would have been pleased by your ingenuity," Carter continued as he again pointed to the side of his head. "Never once has she ever mentioned anything about an underground group or resistance movement. Only victory in the arena. Do you think it can be an Overlord test to see how we will do against Menseratis?"

Han scowled. "Yes," he said in a loud voice, louder than he intended judging by his grimace. "It must be part of their game for the next match."

"That's what I said," said Nikolai.

Carter nodded. "If it is, I don't get it. But I do know this. I'm done training for today. Let's get some sleep. Tomorrow we're fighting some alien combatant who can regenerate himself at will. I don't want this match to be our last."

CHAPTER 18

Her hands clasped together, Zoar-Wrel wrung them over and over, uncertain if she had made a mistake allowing Telmar to go ahead with the plan. The same concerns she felt then spun in her head. What if he was wrong?

She sat down in the only chair in her living quarters. As with most Overlords, though they controlled the lives of billions, their personal possessions focused on the necessities of life—a chair, a sleep chamber, enough protein supplements for a few days, an interactive console for one's work, and not much more. Only their devotion to the High Magistrate, Raxon-Pal, mattered. Anything else considered a distraction was thought of as frivolous.

Frivolous or not, Zoar-Wrel felt the walls of her living quarters draw closer. What would she say to the planetary leaders? Was she leading them into a trap? How would she be remembered by her own people as the one who initiated a revolution against them? Never in the history of the Raxion Union had that ever happened.

"It's all his fault," she said under her breath. If Raxon-Pal had listened to the concerns of those who believed the greatness of their empire lay not on the backs of subdued worlds, but with their cooperation, life would have been pure. Right. But what

Raxon-Pal chose was akin to genocide. Zoar-Wrel had imagined herself in the position of a subdued world, and that had fueled her discomfort with her own peoples' actions. How many species had they made extinct with their retribution ships? Was that the legacy she wished for her own people? She did believe in their greatness, or rather, their potential for greatness, true greatness. With all the destitute planetary systems under their control, how much more would they be remembered for their benevolence if they helped even a fraction of them?

But Raxon-Pal wouldn't hear it. The only legacy he cared about was his own greatness, which he measured by the expanse of his empire. And so he had to be stopped.

She pushed out of her chair and studied her quarters. The lights above felt strangely cold, and distant. The monster on the throne had done this to her. Made her make choices she didn't want to make. And now, she stood on the precipice of her final act of betrayal.

But should she do it? Should she contact the planetary leaders with the message Telmar had given her? Just one word from her lips, and it would set the insurrection into action, or lead to their collective downfall.

A picture of her brother fell into view from across the room. She stared at his stoic face, dressed in his military uniform shortly before he led the attack against the Delfini outpost. She had long ago lost count the number of times they spent together looking up at the stars on warm summer nights, talking about the moral implications of eradicating whole people groups for defying the Raxion Union. And she agreed that what they were doing was right, until she discovered that he had died for a lie. The outpost was not a sanctuary for terrorists and other such revolutionaries, as had been promoted by first tier Sulit-Bay when he served as chief propagandist, but a haven for the poor and oppressed. They dared create a small enclave that rejected the Union's authority, which Raxon-Pal deemed a threat, and had it destroyed. If her brother had not been killed when his fighter accidentally collided with his wingman, she may have never even heard of the outpost, let alone the purpose of its existence.

The longer she stared at his image, the less certain she became about making the transmission.

"What would you do?" she asked him.

Silence.

"I thought so."

Telmar had prayed to his God for guidance, and seemingly gotten it. She felt nothing. Only his assurance about their course of action persuaded her not to postpone the insurrection. People had been known to confuse divine guidance with personal convictions. Had that happened this time too?

The chronograph on her wall chimed for seven cycles. The time for debate had ended. On the other end of the transmission she would soon send out, the planetary leaders waited, just as the plan organized by Taliah had dictated—no open revolt without her final approval.

Zoar-Wrel drew in a deep breath and inputted the command cipher into the console, coded and scrambled. The device chirped and beeped, then fell silent. On the screen, the leaders' names began to appear. Not their real names, of course, in case the signal was picked up by central command, but their designated names. And no visual images, for the same reason.

Once all ninety-seven names appeared, she opened the frequency. "The moon is high in the sky, and will not set again until the sun's first light." She paused a moment. "I repeat, the moon is high in the sky, and will not set again until the sun's first light."

It wasn't the go signal they expected, but a request for confirmation of the leader's support of the plan. If all ninety-seven of them were still behind her, then she would give the final code signal. If even one of them backed out, then the abort signal would be given. She just couldn't bring herself to chance the lives of others if they weren't a hundred percent on board. She at least owed her brother that much.

One by one, the names on the screen turned from blue to green. Her hearts raced with excitement as the leaders offered their support of her, until the last three names. They remained blue. Thinking there might be signal interference, she checked the transceiver. But it was operating within normal parameters. No signal degradation.

Still, the names didn't change.

Her feelings of joy turned to concern. What was taking their leaders so long? Risking detection by one of the sniffer drones assigned to the area, she decided to take a chance and widened the signal for voice activation.

"Tulani Nine, why the delay? Do you add your voice to the chorus?"

She waited. No answer.

"Marsik Rising, do you add your voice to the chorus?"

"Do you?" came the reply.

She stared down at the other names on the screen, all of which had been under the control of the Raxion Union for the past seven generations. If she gave the order to stand down, nothing would change for any of them. What was worse, she wondered. Slavery or death?

Drawing in a short breath, she replied, "We are all members of the same chorus, including the conductor."

Zoar-Wrel lifted her hand from the panel and took a step back, her gaze fixed on the screen. Two of the three names turned green, the last still remained blue. If her support of the plan didn't do its work, she didn't know how she'd respond. Would she still cancel the plan, as she intended?

The final name switched to green.

Like a magnetic pull on her she couldn't resist, Zoar-Wrel moved toward the console and opened signal. "The sun's first light shines in the morning. I repeat, the sun's first light shines in the morning." She had not only set her course, but the course of nine hundred billion lives.

Feeling exhausted by the ordeal, Zoar-Wrel collapsed in her chair. As she sat there, her attention drifted toward the image of her brother. "I hope I haven't just killed us all."

CHAPTER 19

Taliah stood on the platform with Carter, Han, and Nikolai. She didn't say anything, just stared at them. Carter in particular. She turned to leave, then spun around and threw both arms around him. "You take good care of yourself down there. Make this a fight the Overlords will long remember."

Surprised by her unexpected display of affection, Carter hesitated, then slowly brought up his arms. She felt warm, and soft. This was a sensation he could get used to.

Taliah broke away from him, scarcely aware of every pair of eyes on her. "Remember your training." She faced Han and Nikolai. "Stay low, and never take on Menseratis by yourself. He'll finish you off faster than a Niki bird in an eelsin nest if you do."

Her final peace spoken, Taliah nodded at the lift operator, who lowered them into the arena. To her credit, it wasn't much different than the simulation venue she had created. A vast expanse of jungle matched by a vast expanse of rocky terrain unfolded before them. Similarly, the same bamboo trees and cave mouths dotted the landscape. Far, far in the distance, Carter watched the strange regenerative alien being lowered from his platform. He was all alone. Carter felt his fear grow, but he checked it, as his comrades must as well. If they gave into their fears, then the plan laid out by Taliah could fall apart before it had been implemented, which meant the destruction of Earth, and who knew how many other worlds.

When the platform touched the ground, he stepped off and looked at his teammates after taking in their surroundings. "Now that we have a better idea of what the terrain is like, do we hunt him or wait for him to hunt us?"

"If you know anything about me, you know I don't like waiting around," said Nikolai. "Like you Americans say, 'the best defense is a good offense.'"

"But this jungle does not have many familiar scents," Han observed. "And though it is similar in terrain and geography, there are some marked differences, not to mention fighting in heat levels that can kill us if we're exposed to it for too long."

"What will the Overlords do if there's a stalemate between us?" Carter asked. "We're happy on our side of the arctic zone, and Mr. Superman Alien is equally happy in his part of the hot, humid jungle. How long will they wait until a winner is declared?"

"That's a good question," said Han. "Do we want to find out?"

"No," Nikolai barked back. "These arena games have been going on for centuries. I imagine the Overlords have devised some creative ways of making teams that linger too long on one side or another fight to a conclusion. No sense making them angry." He turned and faced Carter. "Care to take the lead?"

"After we construct some weapons." Carter eyed a cluster of bamboo shoots a short distance away. "They should do nicely." What he didn't know was how long he would last before he ended his life, either by his own hand, or the hand of his opponent.

It was a strange thing. He had been on the other side of this equation countless times, and never once gave it a second thought. Like any good hitman, he understood his mark. Studied him. Knew his habits. For several days, even a week, he'd follow him around. Look for an opportunity to move in for the kill, all the while thinking how this person was already dead, and he didn't even know it. Now, death's sinister grip had his eye on him. The only element that made this worth doing was the promise of being revived after the fatal blow had been struck.

Carter laughed to himself. Never in his life had he ever thought of himself as a hero, or better yet, a good person. It seemed Clarence and the priest he befriended had more of an impact on him than he realized.

"Before we go commando into Menseratis' side of the arena, we should make as many spears and knives as we can effectively carry. From what Taliah's said, he's going to be a tough guy to kill."

Han and Nikolai nodded their approvals.

Finding some rocks in the area, they banged them together several times before three shards could be used for cutting and sharpening.

Carter had never visited a country in the tropics, so he couldn't say for sure if the bamboo on this planet was the same as on Earth. It cut easily enough, and its rigid structure formed sharpened edges that could eviscerate its victim without much difficulty.

Not wanting to be weighed down, the three decided to carry two spears each, one for each hand, and a hand-held version that would act like a knife. What Menseratis had in mind, they could only guess.

When they were nearly done, Nikolai knelt down and drew a rough outline of the arena geography. In the middle, he positioned a couple of stones and some twigs. "From what I saw on the platform before we dropped, a high ridge separates our side from his. Lots of trees and jungle growth in between. In Menseratis' part of the arena, he has the higher ground, which is unfortunate. And not much plant growth, no doubt the result of the high heat. If he uses the geography the way I would if I were him, he can easily see us coming a long way off."

His hand pressed against his mouth, Han knelt down and studied the crude model. "Never forget we have the advantage of numbers. Menseratis can only be in one place at one time."

"As far as we know," Carter interrupted.

"If he had some kind of teleportation ability," Nikolai said, "Taliah would have told us."

Han picked up a twig and drew a line in the sand from their position to the last known location of their opponent. "Regeneration seems to be his primary skill. Which would make sense—he'd wait for us rather than fight in an environment that works against him. Be in control of your surroundings. That's how you win battles."

As Carter studied the straight line Han drew, a strategy emerged in his mind. "You talked about the three-to-one ratio we have against Menseratis. Like you said, he can only be one place at a time. What if we turned the tables on him?"

"What do you mean?" Han asked.

"We do the same with one of us. Give him an easy target to attack."

Nikolai's brow furrowed. "You mean bait."

"That's right." Carter split the line into three parts with his finger. "Though the setting is very different, I think the strategy we used in the aerial battle will work here as well. One of us sweeps around on the left, one in the middle, and the other on the right. Menseratis goes for the easy, obvious target in the middle, and the other two close in and cut him off. It's a classic pincer movement that can bring us a quick victory."

"And then what happens to you?"

Han's question cut deep into Carter. "Then we initiate the next phase of the plan." He couldn't bring himself to say they'd have to kill him, compliments of the listening device in his head.

Grabbing his spears, Nikolai stood upright. "I say it's a plan worth trying."

"Since it was my idea, I should be the bait." Carter looked at his teammates, whose silence morphed into a de facto yes. "Good."

Both spears clutched in his hands, Carter took the lead. It didn't take long for them to get enfolded by the jungle. If this had been an old movie, they'd have been slashing at palm fronds and bushes with machetes. Fortunately for all three, enough of a path existed for them to navigate their way toward their objective. As they did, strange animal sounds flittered about them. Some were high-pitched calls that sounded like birds, while others were low grunts made by a number of unseen creatures. Carter could only imagine what they looked like, and how dangerous they might be.

They had gone several hundred meters, when Carter suddenly stopped. The basis of their plan rested on the assumption that Menseratis waited for them on his side. What if he didn't? What if he had snuck into their territory, and was waiting for them to fall into his trap? With all the jungle growth around them, a hundred traps could have been laid, and they'd never see them.

"What's wrong?" Nikolai asked.

At his question, the jungle turned quiet, like a sound switch had been thrown.

"You see something?" Han came alongside Carter, his spears at the ready.

"No," Carter replied. "That's the problem. We have no idea where our opponent is, and so we shouldn't go traipsing through the jungle like we don't have a care in the world. It's that kind of thinking that can get us killed."

"Then what do you suggest?"

Even Carter didn't know. He recognized the obvious danger, but as far as a solution went, he didn't have one.

Nikolai's demeanor darkened. "If you're having doubts, I should take the lead."

Though it wasn't a challenge to Carter's authority, it still felt like one. "No. We stick with the plan. I'm merely pointing the recklessness of going straight for the other side without considering the possibility that Menseratis isn't where we expect him to be."

"Agreed," Han said. "We continue forward, but with caution."

They walked for another hour, but it felt like they were no closer to the other side of the arena than when they had started. One difference, however, did emerge during their journey. The further they went, the thicker the jungle became.

The vast grove of trees, fifty or so meters high, with their bushy limbs stretched up towards the heavens, blocked out all but the faintest hints of sunlight. Spaced twenty paces from each other, the red-barked behemoths stood like silent sentinels in a place that had known almost constant conflict for countless years. But here, in this place of shade and silence, time itself seemed to stand fixed. If it weren't for the sounds of their feet clomping against the hardened dirt and the chatter of animals, there would be no noise whatsoever.

Carter both enjoyed and feared the forest. It brought a sense of calm to him on the one hand, and a feeling of fear on the other. Serenity, like most things, was a mirage, and when one found himself in a place that manifested such a particular feeling, it usually meant unseen dangers lingered nearby.

A high-pitched sound darted past his ear. Thinking it was a small insect he waved his hand into the air. That same sound flew by his other ear. Carter instinctively jerked his head back. It was then that he noticed Han and Nikolai doing the same thing, until something long and pointed struck Nikolai in the neck.

"Oww," he said, then plucked it out and stared at the tiny dart -like thing. His eyes suddenly rolled back, and he fell onto the ground, unconscious.

"Stinger darts!" Han shouted.

"Blast!" Carter replied with the same alarm in his voice. He bent down low, looking for a way of escape. "We've got to get out of here before they get us all."

A vine dropped down from above and landed next to Nikolai. When it missed him, the vine shot up into the air for a few seconds, this time landing on the other side of him.

"Get Nikolai away from that tree," Carter ordered, "or that vine will lift him up to the branches, and probably make a meal out of him."

Han leapt forward with his spears and charged at the vine. He landed a short distance away from their woozy compatriot. The vine reacted to Han's arrival, and went after him. It wrapped around his right wrist, and attempted to do the same to his left. But Han anticipated the plant's move, and jerked it out of the way. Reaching back for his hand weapon, Han clutched it tight and drove the point into the vine still wrapped around his wrist. A high-pitched cry of pain rose above the jungle floor, and the vine loosened its grip on Han before recoiling into the canopy above.

Carter reached down and grabbed Nikolai. "Hurry," he said, "before that thing makes another grab at us."

Han didn't have to be told twice. He practically yanked up Nikolai with Carter's assistance and bolted forward through the jungle.

All around them, the sounds of darts whizzed past their head and ears. Neither Carter nor Han could do anything but keep low and hope for the best.

When it seemed like exhaustion would overtake them, a faint halo of light shone in the distance. Barely perceptible at first, the hazy glow grew in intensity, until the jagged outline of a ridge appeared.

"Keep going," Carter shouted between winded breaths. "We're almost out."

Han broke through the edge of the forest first, followed by Carter, Nikolai between them. Feeling like they were no longer in danger, Carter stopped. He collapsed on the ground, sucking in lungs full of air. Next to him, Han did the same, though his breaths were shallower.

After several minutes, Carter thought it prudent to check on

Nikolai. Was he still alive?

His face was pale white, and his eyes, red and swollen, looked straight up at the sky with a deathlike stare. Fearing the worst, he checked the Russian's pulse. It was there. Faint, but still beating. Carter let out a sigh of relief.

All at once, Nikolai bolted up. "Nooo!" he shouted. Then looked around.

"Nikolai."

"Where am I?" Nikolai asked. "What happened?" He lay back down on the ground, catching his breath.

"We were attacked by a tree that shot darts at us. Do you remember?"

Nikolai shook his head.

"One of them hit you. I guess they're tipped with poison that knocks you out. Then it dropped down a vine to grab you, which we assumed intended to lift you up to make a meal out of you."

Though Carter didn't think it possible, Nikolai's face grew even whiter. His mouth contorted into a strange shape, and he turned away. Several deep heaves ejected his breakfast.

Just as quickly as the purging started, it stopped. A sideways glance indicated Nikolai's embarrassment, though Carter didn't think he had anything to be embarrassed about. Throwing up was obviously the result of the dart's poison.

"Sorry about that," Nikolai apologized after he wiped off his mouth with his sleeve.

Han patted Nikolai's shoulder. "Understandable," he said, "given the circumstances."

Nikolai took a look around. "Where are we?"

"At the border between your side and mine," an otherworldly voice declared from above.

Carter's head snapped up in the direction of the ridge, followed by Han's and Nikolai's. There, standing on the top, was Menseratis, a lone spear in his hand.

He brought the tip forward and pointed it at the three. "Who shall go first?"

* * *

Taliah couldn't keep her eyes off the giant collage of view screens in the observation room. Only weeks before, thirty-two trainers had been allowed in the building. Now, four remained. Taliah had been in this situation often, only this time, her heart felt as if it were pounding in her throat.

"Care for some Suqui and berries?" asked the familiar silky voice of Zelroth Klin of Tatos Prime. The trainer who almost without exception found his way into the final four. Everything he said was always tinged with subtle insult. It was as if his tongue were a whip that beat her down if she didn't put up her defenses.

"No thank you," she said, hoping he would go away.

"My, my, what a difficult match your three men face. But odds are at least one of your men will make it, don't you think?"

"I am hoping for two," she said in a placating tone.

"Carter, for sure. He's the man who's taken your heart."

Her gaze left the screen and found Zelroth Klin's two shadowed eyes watching her. His long, pale face danced with the flickering colors of the screen.

"What did you say?"

Zelroth chuckled. "Excuse my poor language skills. I only meant he's learned your fighting skills well. The passion and zeal you have for each match, he has made them his own. Your heart has been made his." He took a step back and studied her. "Of course, that is a very attractive character trait. Hard not to be drawn to an off-worlder like that."

Taliah turned and faced the screen. *Go away, pest.*

Still, something in his voice insinuated more than idle specu-lation. Had he observed Carter and her? Zelroth had been a sneak before. It had not been uncommon to find him observing her trainees outside the arena in order to get a sense of their tricks and personalities. Could he have seen her and Carter's last embrace through the transparent walls of her team's cell? Or was he simply guessing based on psychology? Zelroth adored psy-choanalysis. That was one of his strengths as a trainer, finding the mental weaknesses of opponents and then training his men in such a way as to exploit them.

"What do you want, Zelroth? I know you're not chatting with me for any other reason than to get in my head."

Out of the corner of her eye, she caught a thin smile slip across his face.

"I am being civil, so should you." He paused, as if his words were reasonable. "Like Carter, Menseratis has heart too. That is why he's lasted so long. I find it interesting so many... kind-hearted fighters made it this far into the games."

A shout sounded from across the room where the other arena match took place.

"Oh, my," said Zelroth, "another of Sintalae's men gone. Now both of their teams are down to a single fighter. One on one in the poison swamp. We've seen that end in disaster more than once, haven't we Taliah?"

She couldn't help but be brought into the past by Zelroth's words, to three separate matches where she and Zelroth's team both perished as they fought to kill their opponents, while at the same time survive the poison swamp littered with deadly traps. Of course, the arena her team fought in was littered with nearly as many dangers. Nikolai had found that out the hard way with a tree dart to the neck.

"Your man, Menseratis has heart, you say?" said Taliah. "That must really annoy you."

"I prefer heartless killers, but if I have to have one with feelings and emotion, at least I got one who can heal himself. That helps make up for the softness."

Taliah didn't respond, hoping Zelroth would leave her alone. Carter, Han, and Nikolai were all deliberating on what should be done about the challenge Menseratis gave them. A heaviness bore on her soul as she watched Carter's face. There was no fear in his eyes, though she knew it lay underneath his calm mask. She remembered the embrace she'd given him before the arena match. His strong arms held her for that brief moment. And then she remembered his touch in the medical room, when he agreed to take on her desperate plan. She'd never known bravery like that. He was a good man. The Overlords had made a mistake bringing him here. If everything went according to plan, she and billions of others would forever be indebted to him. She was the one who asked him to do this horrible thing. To die. And it was to her that he said yes.

He had trusted her, even though he still barely knew her. Her plan had to succeed. For his sake. She would be heartbroken if something went wrong when he died, and he could not be brought back.

The thought nearly crushed her, and she flung it from her mind, lest it bring her to tears before Zelroth, who stood before her, watching her face.

"What are you doing?" barked Taliah with anger. "Can you not give me some privacy to watch the match?"

"You are up to something, Taliah. The Overlords know. They've come to me and asked me about you."

Her eyes jumped to Zelroth. She searched his face. Why else would he say something like that unless it were true?

Still, she played coy, for caution's sake. "What are you talking about?"

"Foolish, Taliah. You are so weak-hearted, just like the men we've been discussing. Joining up with a rebellion against the biggest, most powerful force in the universe. That's exactly the kind of stupidity that living by one's heart gets you. You should have simply sought power within your life's station and risen where you were. But perhaps a heartless being like me could help you. Tell me, does this rebellion actually have a chance?"

She stared at him. Was this a trap? Clearly, the Overlords had come to him, but was he working for them, or simply reaching out to her?

She'd truly be a fool to assume the latter.

"I am not part of any rebellion. Did the Overlords really come to you, or are you simply trying to get under my skin?" Short answers. Always the most effective way of deflecting the truth.

Zelroth's eyebrows drew together like spider legs closing in on a fly. "They came to me. They showed me clips and recordings of you. And not only you. Now tell me, is this rebellion actually dangerous? Because if it is, I want to be on the winning side."

Taliah was at a loss for words. How could she continue to

posture and pretend like she didn't know anything when he clearly had been approached by the Overlords? And that meant they knew about her. But if true, why was she still alive?

A cry sounded from the corner of the room where the screens showing the poison swamp glowed.

"Yesss!" Zelroth hissed. "Just as we were hoping."

A replay showed on the screen. The two men struggled, each holding a knife, trying to wrestle the other to the ground and finish off their opponent. But they stumbled onto a poisonous quicksand pit. The last image was of the two men disappearing beneath the glowing sand. That meant the match between her men and Zelroth's was the last one. But that created a problem. Her plan's success depended on time, the longer the better. Carter had to be taken to medical, have the monitor device in his head surgically removed, then during low personnel hours, go to the Positron Center and meet up with Zoar-Wrel. There, he'd be on his own to shut down the energy source that powered every ship and weapon within the Overlord's empire.

But time had just been taken from their hands. Zelroth knew, which meant the Overlords probably did as well. There would be no final match a day or two from now that would distract the Overlords. The Positron Center would not be low staffed.

Taliah's heart began to race. It felt like the plan was falling apart, and she couldn't stop it. But how could she back out now? There was no way for her to get a message to Carter.

She rose from her chair. As much as it pained her, she had to tell Zoar-Wrel the rebellion would have to be postponed. Another thought slipped into her head. If the Overlords did know, she couldn't go to Zoar-Wrel, not without jeopardizing her friend who had risked everything, not to mention the future of the rebellion. Indecision tugged at Taliah's emotions.

She turned back to Zelroth. His eyes studied her as they always did. And as usual, it made her skin crawl. What other choice did she have but to admit to the enemy before her that his information about the rebellion was true? If she did, Taliah hoped she would find out what the Overlords told him and how much they knew.

"Yes," she whispered. "The rebellion is broader and stronger than the Raxion Union suspects. And it will bring the Overlord's empire to its knees."

Zelroth's eyes lit with excitement. "Ah! So it is true." He sniggered in that awkward way only members of Tatos Prime could do. "So, Taliah, if I am to align myself with your rebellion, I need to know for sure that you really can win. As you know, I am heartless. I only care about being on the side that has the power. So tell me, what is your plan?"

Though his words voiced the opposite, Taliah was certain Zelroth worked for the Overlords. And this was nothing more than an act of deception which would trick her into revealing who was involved in the insurrection. Raxon Pal had used similar tactics before. Now it made sense why she was still alive. The knowledge she possessed as the leader of the rebellion. Once she gave up what she knew, or it became apparent she would never talk, her usefulness would come to a sudden end, and so would she.

Time. Time was what Carter needed. And the only way she could give it to him was the perception of cooperation. "First, tell me what the Overlords said. What do they know about me?"

"They have some vid evidence and recordings of you talking with co-conspirators. What else can I say?"

"Why haven't they arrested me yet?"

Zelroth shrugged. "Perhaps they want to... draw more information from you. That way they can discover additional members within your so-called rebellion, cast their net wide and catch the lot of you."

Taliah thought his answer clever. Expose the truth of the situation as a means of gaining her trust. When in fact, it was another carefully crafted act of deception on his part. With trust comes cooperation, and cooperation leads to information. "And is that what you're doing right now, Zelroth? Working for them? Drawing information out of me?" She could play the same game as him.

The left side of his lips rose. "Taliah, I would never sell you out. At least, not before I discovered whether or not you really did have power. Do you think I like living as a slave? Never a day goes by that I don't think about what I really am—a trained animal that does the bidding of its master."

Taliah glared at him. "Do you really think a slave rebellion has any chance against the entire Raxion Union? I have a hard time believing you would ever think this."

Zelroth's eyes said it all. She saw the humorous light in them. "I think it's possible. So are you going to tell me your plan or not?"

With the force of the fighter that lived inside her, Taliah's fist struck Zelroth's chin—the dangerous girl well known back on her home world of Axinar IV.

Zelroth stumbled backwards, and grabbed the side of his face. A knife appeared in his hands. "This is going to be a pleasure," he said, his voice razor sharp.

He crouched low, then in an instant, sprang towards her. She blocked Zelroth's knife hand with her right wrist, and brought a knee up to his face, so that the full force of her body slammed against it.

He cried out feebly as she stole the knife from his limp fingers, then drove the butt of it into his skull.

Zelroth's crumpled unconscious form lay still on the floor. Taliah glanced up at the screen and took one long look at Carter. She saw he was alone now, climbing up towards Menseratis' position. Her heart ached. He was about to sacrifice himself, now for nothing? The rebellion was falling apart. She had to warn Zoar-Wrel. Otherwise, the entire uprising could be crushed before it began.

Taliah spun around and took a step towards the door, then froze.

Five figures had entered the room. They came towards her slowly. Three of them were Overlord guards carrying shock sticks. The other two were powerful Overlords she knew well.

Telmin-Kai and Sulit-Bay.

Feeling them move closer, Taliah counted every breath she took. They couldn't be allowed to take her alive. They would use the bore worms on her. For a time, she could resist the pain, but for how long? An hour, a minute, a day? Sooner or later, they would discover the plan. That, she could never permit. With sadness, Taliah's hand slowly moved for her suicide vial. This was it. She was going to die. And the rebellion would fall apart.

Her fingertips brushed the cold surface and she readied herself.

Suddenly, a heavy object struck the back of her head. Pain shot down her spine. She lost her grip on the vial as she turned to defend herself.

Zelroth stood with a metal object in his hand, a sneer on his face.

Her vision swirled from the blow to her head. Desperately, she tried to retrieve the vial which had fallen to the ground. There it was, right beneath her. She fell to her knees and grabbed it.

But the metal object cracked against her skull a second time, knocking her to the floor. Everything spun. Her stomach lurched from the pain and darkness stole away her last desperate thought of the vial and pulled her into the realm of nightmares.

The bore worms. They would use the bore worms.

CHAPTER 20

Carter had chosen to take the most dangerous route. Straight up the hill. Straight to Menseratis. Han went around to the left, while Nikolai moved to the right. It would take his teammates longer to reach their enemy this way, but if Carter was going to get himself killed, he was the one who had to take all the risks.

Just above him, Carter took hold of a rocky crag to pull himself past a steep cleft in the rocks. His path was almost entirely a vertical one. Truly, it was a foolish route to take, but it did provide a tempting target for Menseratis. One he couldn't imagine his opponent resisting, even if the man knew that Carter's two other teammates were closing in to surround him.

Another large boulder loomed overhead. Carter grabbed a handhold, and stabilized himself with his left foot, traversed another difficult stretch of vertical cliff. If he fell now, he was high enough up to guarantee his own death. The thought of falling terrified him. Then again, so was the thought of dying in any fashion.

"What are you doing?" came a voice above.

Carter glanced up. Menseratis frowned down at him.

"Coming to kill you of course," said Carter.

"You're coming to kill me? It looks more like you're trying to get yourself killed. I think the chances of you making it to the top are hard enough on their own, but then, if I were to begin dropping rocks on your head, I'd say your chances of coming up to kill me would be at zero. So again, I ask you, what are you doing? I know you are not mentally impaired. My trainer, Zelroth Klin, gave me a very detailed report on your psychology."

Carter studied the man's face. Somehow, the fact that Menseratis made the time to talk instead of trying to kill him gave Carter respect for this new enemy. He didn't seem like the cold-blooded killers Carter had met in the other matches. With them, there had been no talking at all. Only a focused intent on eliminating their opponents.

"I must say," said Cater. "I appreciate you not killing me yet. On my world, that would be considered very, um, considerate."

"You interest me, Carter. Tell me now, why have you chosen this route? It is so poor, I can't help but wonder at it."

"Perhaps I am simply trying to distract you while I allow my two teammates to pinch you in from opposite sides."

"Well yes, that is of course what is happening. I am not unaware of the direction Han and Nikolai went. But, for you, either you are recklessly brave, or you are trying to commit suicide." He pointed toward his left. "Do you see this rock?"

Carter reached out and gripped a jagged piece of rock sticking from the dirt. It came loose in his hand, which caused his body to slide backward. Pebbles and dirt rained down on his head from where the stone had come loose, and he drug his hands like rakes against the loose surface. Faster and faster he slid, until he managed to grab a protruding stone with one hand.

"Hold on just one moment," said Carter, hoping the seemingly polite alien above would continue his courteousness. Carter managed to find a second hand hold, and finally hefted himself back up to a safer position, pinning his feet in a wedge of sturdy rock.

Glancing up, Carter saw the rock that Menseratis had mentioned. It was quite large, a little bigger than a softball. If thrown down at him, it certainly could prove very painful—if not fatal.

Menseratis knelt by the cliff's edge. The closer he moved toward him, the more Carter had a chance to take in the alien's form. Though Menseratis appeared human-like in some ways, his skin displayed a kind of sheen that made it look damp. His eyes were also larger than someone from Earth, and brightly colored. Multi-colored would be more accurate. Reds, blues, and golds shone brightly in the afternoon sun. Menseratis' hair looked normal enough, except that it vibrated at the slightest movement.

Standing six feet tall by his estimation, and weighing in the neighborhood of a hundred and seventy-five pounds, the alien looked no more menacing than a common Joe you'd meet on the street. But Taliah had warned them repeatedly about his fighting skills, and his ability to regenerate from the most severe of wounds. Though unexpectedly cordial, Carter reminded himself he was dealing with a killer, and an effective one at that.

"I am going to have to kill you, Carter, though I wish with all my heart that I didn't have to. These games disgust me."

Carter met his opponent's eyes. The shape of the man's face was strange, different, but human. Just like Taliah. Her face was also strange, exotic and other-worldly, but it was also beautiful, and human.

"We share that sentiment in common," said Carter. "It is the Overlords my heart burns against, not you or any of the other men I've faced in these games of theirs."

Menseratis nodded. "My problem is, with you, it is far from a fair fight, and something inside me cannot stand the idea of hurtling rocks down at you until you fall to your death. If you and I were squaring off, each with a knife in hand, that would be another matter. But this, it feels despicable."

Carter stared at the man. Hot wind whipped at his hands and legs as he clung to the face of the cliff wall. Carter felt angry. More angry than he'd been in any of the other arena matches. Nikolai and Han would have to kill this man. And more than that, Carter needed this man to kill him. And curse it all, Menseratis had to be the most decent opponent they had faced. That threw a wrench into his plan.

Carter wished he could just blurt out the truth. About the rebellion. But then, the Overlords had placed the recorder in his skull; it would relay any words he said straight to their listening ears.

What could he do?

"I'm not afraid of dying," said Carter. "One of us must be killed. One of our worlds must go free while the other's is enslaved. Who is to say which world is more deserving?"

Carter wiped the sweat from his brow. The heat was staggering. The bottle of water slung over his shoulder was getting low.

"My trainer, Zelroth Klin, tells me you have grown close to your trainer. He saw it as a weakness I might exploit. My trainer is a twisted individual. But is it true? Have you in this short time found love?"

The question surprised Carter. Though he had not thought through his feelings for Taliah, they had found a foothold over the course of the arena matches. The lingering touches. The embraces. But was that love? He thought of the request she had made, to join the rebellion in giving up his life. It was such a preposterous thing to ask him, but he knew why she did. Because she had grown to trust him. And that trust had given him the strength to say 'yes.'

"Yes, I do have feelings for her," said Carter. "I—" He had to be careful what words he chose. "I have come to trust her with my life."

Menseratis stood. "I imagine she is watching you now on the view screen. I will not kill you like this." He glanced toward his left, as if he saw someone coming. "Farewell, Carter. Next time I see you, have a weapon in hand. I will not kill an unarmed man."

With that last statement, Menseratis left the cliff's edge. Carter grimaced. All the fight in him had left. How was he supposed to help Han and Nikolai kill a man like that? An honorable man.

An idea passed into his mind—a possible way of solving this conundrum. He clutched onto the thought like a breath of hope and slowly resumed ascending the cliff.

* * *

Nikolai watched as Menseratis' figure moved closer to him through the undergrowth. This was going to be perfect. The spear in his hand was drawn back like a catapult ready to be loosed. Han's presence had spooked their enemy just as Nikolai had hoped. A slit in the fronds of a huge purple veined plant was a near perfect observation point.

Menseratis wouldn't even know what hit him.

Sweat stung Nikolai's eyes as it dripped down from his hair.

His entire face was beaded and wet. The heat was nearly unbearable.

A subtle swishing noise rose from the jungle floor as Menseratis neared. Nikolai felt the tingle of excitement as he waited like a poised statue for the right moment. Slowly, Menseratis came around a large trunk into plain view, his steps slowing, almost as if he sensed danger. Menseratis raised his spear, listening.

With all of his might, Nikolai hurled the spear.

Menseratis' head sprang to his right, toward the sound of Nikolai, but too late. The spear shaft sunk into the man's chest, and he cried out in agony, stumbling back, then falling.

Nikolai drew the bamboo knife and moved to finish the job. In the distance, Han made his way through the dense jungle toward his position. Nikolai hurried to his downed enemy. He knew Menseratis could regenerate, so time was of the essence. Equally important, he wanted to brag to Han of Russian superiority when it came to ambush. Nothing like an opportunity to gloat as a means of upping their motivation for victory.

With one hand Menseratis clutched the spear, grimacing, as if trying to remove it. Nikolai raised his knife as he neared. There was no way that thing was coming out. Nikolai wondered at how the man was still alive. The head of the spear was lodged in his upper left breast, right where the heart was. But then Nikolai realized, this was not a human from Earth. Perhaps Menseratis' heart resided elsewhere in his body.

No matter. There were other vital points.

Nikolai leapt on Menseratis, moving his knife toward his opponent's neck, when suddenly he produced a bamboo blade of his own. Nikolai realized his mistake, and tried to roll off, but too late. Menseratis' blade clutched tight in his hand struck between Nikolai's upper two ribs below his left breast.

Nikolai gasped.

"If only you had studied our anatomy as I have studied yours," said Menseratis. "You would have known my heart is in my right breast, unlike yours which is in the left."

Nikolai collapsed beside the alien, feeling his life leaving his body. He stared at the foliage in the distance and knew he'd be dead before Han ever reached him.

Menseratis, the spear still sticking out of his chest, rammed the back of it into a tree, driving the shaft through his body. Each slamming blow caused the alien to scream in pain. When the point finally came through, the alien pulled the shaft out with an agonized groan.

Nikolai closed his eyes. This man was a terror. He would be impossible to kill. Han would die. Carter would die.

Perhaps Earth could still be saved. Perhaps...

Nikolai's last image was of his niece's birthday party back in Korolyov. The children's smiles grew large as they chased one another around the vineyards of his sister's country home. The children's laughter took Nikolai home.

* * *

"Go in peace," said Han, kneeling beside Nikolai's still body. Tears came down his face as the finality of death pervaded the air he breathed. "Your soul will be missed, my Russian friend." Han kept his eyes up, only glancing down at Nikolai for the briefest of moments.

Menseratis was not far off. He stood, watching Han, almost as if studying him.

Han raised himself slowly from the ground and stared back at his opponent. The alien pointed at his own chest, then bowed, as if showing respect. Han nodded as he bowed in return. The alien nodded in reply. The two stood facing each other, silent, for what seemed to Han like minutes. But even without words, much passed between him and the opposing fighter. Finally, Han turned back cautiously toward the cliff where he'd last seen Carter.

Their enemy was far deadlier, and more honorable than he cared to deal with. Nikolai had skewered him, and yet Menseratis somehow managed to kill his Russian friend while impaled by a spear. But for some reason, Han could not find anger in his heart at Menseratis.

Only sadness.

Nikolai was dead. Not because Menseratis killed him. But because the Overlords forced Menseratis to kill him. That was what Han mustn't forget. His wrath and anger had to spring from the proper source. From the ones who pitted men against one another in the hopes of gaining military strategies and skills that would further their empire's expansion.

The Overlords.

Those were the beings Han wanted to drive his spear through.

To hate Menseratis... that would be to hate himself.

CHAPTER 21

Taliah woke slowly, her vision fading in and out as she tried to open her eyes despite the pain throbbing at the back of her head. She did her best to recall the last series of events. Carter was climbing the cliff wall, straight toward Menseratis. She remembered watching with horror as he did exactly what he was supposed to do. But inside, her chest roiled like an angry sea. Though she'd seen thousands of deaths in the arenas for the last three generations, she couldn't bear to see Carter's. She had grown too close to him—and more than that, he was placing his trust in her—she was the reason he was going to die.

The only reassurance that made a difference for her was that he would be resurrected. As long as their plan remained intact.

Her eyes suddenly shot open, and she tried to sit up. Something restrained her. A tight strip of metal strapped her head down, her hands and legs likewise bound in place.

Suddenly, her last moments returned to her.

...The fight with Zelroth Klin. The appearance of Telmin-Kai and Sulit-Bay.

Her loss of the suicide vial.

"Hello Taliah," said a voice that was unmistakably made from the stunted throat of an Overlord.

Sulit-Bay's face appeared over her, followed by Telmin-Kai's.

"We are going to make this brief and simple," said Sulit-Bay. "Tell us everything about the rebellion you are a part of, or you will find your body playing host to these little beauties."

Telmin-Kai held up a transparent container. Inside, the squirming bodies of bore worms wriggled against the sides.

"These are newly-hatched bore worms. They take much longer than their adult counterparts to consume a victim from within. I figured you have much to tell us, so perhaps a week of slowly being eaten alive, day and night, would give you time enough to tell us every detail of your rebellion. And of course, for every verifiable piece of information you give us, we will gladly give you five minutes of relief with a shot of Dyxthomine serum. But of course, it doesn't have to come to that."

Telmin-Kai placed the small container of bore worms on her forehead. "I like you, Taliah. I might even reinstate you as a trainer, depending upon your cooperation, of course."

The worm's writhing bodies made her stomach churn.

"We are giving you thirty minutes to think about your choice," said Telmin-Kai. "Remember, once we give you the bore worms, your only hope will be to tell all and receive the pain-relieving serum. Or, enjoy all the rich nerve ending nibblings of these little ones for days on end. I've heard no one has gone more than a day before doing what it takes to receive the serum. But then, why go through all that when you could take Sulit-Bay's generous offer? You could be back in the arena matches for the next cycle of games, all this business about rebellion put in the past."

Sulit-Bay stroked the side of her face with his cold finger-like appendages.

"We'll return shortly, dear. I am looking forward to hearing all you have to say... one way, or another."

Taliah heard a door hiss as it slid shut, and she was alone in the room.

Alone, and without any hope other than the meager chance that the rebellion's plan might somehow come to pass. But that would require her to delay, and she could only do that for so long. Once she was given the bore worms...

* * *

Sulit-Bay looked intensely at Telmin-Kai. "Soon we will know names and timelines. We will crush them. Utterly crush them."

"Have you discovered anything from the device you placed on Carter?" asked Telmin-Kai.

"Nothing. But we'll watch and wait. Chances are, he won't live through this match with Zelroth Klin's fighter."

Telmin-Kai nodded. "I thought it odd how bold he's suddenly become. Carter has always been cautious in his other fights. But this time, he appeared to be acting recklessly. I feel something strange is going on."

Sulit-Bay chortled a high pitched sound, the equivalent of a shrug. "Keep an eye on him, then."

His eyes turned to a screen on the wall where the arena match was displayed.

"Are you really going to reinstate Taliah if she talks?" asked Telmin-Kai.

Another chortle sounded from Sulit-Bay's throat, only low in tone and pitch. "Yes. I would. But she won't cooperate. She's too much of a fighter. I'm afraid it will be the bore worms for her. But that will be enjoyable in and of itself. Then we'll get to see how much fight she truly has."

* * *

Carter and Han stood on the cliff's edge looking into the shadows of the jungle. Carter took a long swig of water, streams of sweat running down his face. He felt like he could barely catch his breath, his lungs despising the hot, sweltering air being taken in. The exertion of traversing the vertical cliff had left his entire body aching and sore.

And his heart was heavy. Nikolai, dead? The Russian had always been antagonistic, but that jeering playfulness had grown on him. And he could see it in Han's eyes, too. Grief, defeat.

"What do we do now?" asked Han. "Menseratis is not the kind of enemy I want to fight. He may have killed Nikolai, but it was in self-defense, and the way in which he looked at me afterwards. It was almost as if he were saying with his eyes, *I am sorry.*"

Carter nodded. "Respectful and deadly." He paused. "He could have killed me too, but he didn't."

"What do you mean?" asked Han.

"He had a rock in his hand that would have knocked me off the cliff, but he never threw it. Said it wasn't right to kill a man like that."

Carter wanted badly to communicate with Han without fear of the Overlords hearing. There was no sense in delaying the inevitable—he had to make Menseratis kill him—but then, Han's chances against their skilled opponent were slim. And beyond his desire to see Han move to the next match, the mercy shown to him by Menseratis made him wish that somehow both men could survive until the Overlords were overthrown.

Carter glanced up at the sky. High overhead, the platform holding the Overlord dignitaries floated like a cloud. Carter imagined them watching through binocular-like devices. To them, they were like gladiators. Entertainment.

"Han, I am going for Menseratis. You do what you want with that."

Han's eyes held no emotion as they searched Carter's. A nod signaled that he understood. Carter was going to his death. Han could choose to use that to whatever advantage he wanted.

He reached out and embraced Carter. "You will defeat the enemy. You will have ultimate victory, my friend."

The words were full of cryptic meaning. They both knew who the enemy was.

Not Menseratis.

* * *

Carter walked swiftly through the foliage, pushing the large fronds from his path, ducking beneath vines and low hanging branches. His water container was down to one last swig. He wondered what the Overlords thought of his sudden boldness. Did this appease them somehow? Excite them? Or were they pure strategists who found such gutsy moves the choices of fools?

But God has chosen the foolish things of the world to put to shame the wise. Carter had heard that somewhere back on Earth. The maxim had sounded so ridiculous when he first heard it. But it had made an impression on him. Why else would he have remembered it?

Then it came to him. It was a passage of scripture spoken by the priest at Clarence's church. While Carter sat in a pew and waited for him to leave so he could put a bullet through his head, those outrageous words had come rolling from the priest's mouth. They were so strange, and yet, the very oddness of them had captured his attention.

Those words now felt fitting. He was going to do something that seemed above all else a very foolish thing. Getting oneself intentionally killed. It went against his code as a cartel hitman. But that same code also taught him the importance of faithfulness and loyalty. Without Earth, where would his faithfulness and loyalty lie? Himself? How little indeed did he value those he knew if he put his safety and protection above everyone else's. His self-sacrifice came a little easier knowing that Taliah's plan was quite brilliant. She had the right pieces to make it work. Two Overlords who had turned, one a medical worker who had the power to revive a dead man. For all the brains the Overlords had, this was such a strange and foolish plan. It could hardly be their fault for succumbing to it.

Carter only hoped things were still running smoothly outside the arena. He thought of Taliah, watching him now. He longed to hold her in his arms once this was all over. As he walked on, he found himself rethinking Menseratis' question about loving Taliah. He didn't really know what love was. Had never loved a girl in his life. Had only been an assassin. Perhaps Taliah truly had feelings for him beyond a momentary need to help her and the rebellion. That thought put an extra step to Carter's pace. A prayer escaped his lips. A prayer asking for that very opportunity. To see Taliah again and find out her feelings. How deep did they run for him?

"Going somewhere?" came a voice to Carter's left.

He spun and found Menseratis standing not far off beside the large trunk of a tree, his arms folded.

Carter drew his bamboo knife. "Hello again."

"Where's your other teammate... Han?"

Carter took in the stoic look on the alien man's face. Was it characteristic of all the people from his home world? "I imagine he's somewhere not far off. But I honestly don't know."

"Don't know?" asked Menseratis, more than a little surprised, judging by his tone. "That is a strange plan. For a team who's gotten this far, I am perplexed by your lack of strategy. Tell me, what is your plan? If it's to confuse me, you have certainly succeeded."

Again, Carter longed for that cursed device to be gone. If he could speak plainly to the man before him, so much could be said.

"Can we make a bargain?" Carter asked. "If I kill you, I promise to make it as quick as I know how. But if you kill me, would you promise to do the same?"

Menseratis appraised him in silence.

"I can agree to that." He cocked his head to one side. "I take it you are not going to answer my initial question about your odd strategy. Of all the species on my home world, my people have the most adept hearing. I can hear your teammate, Han, trying to walk silently through the undergrowth. He is very far off, certainly not within range to help you." His head swayed back to a balance point between his shoulders. "A very perplexing strategy. Almost makes me hesitate to kill you."

It was now or never, thought Carter. If he were not restricted in what he could say, he would be happy to talk to Menseratis all day. But considering the circumstances, he wanted to get this last part over with quickly. His one relieving thought amidst the swirling fear and apprehension was that he knew Menseratis would keep his word. The alien man would kill him quickly.

Carter moved towards his adversary. In response, he unfolded his arms, but remained fixed. Carter searched the man's belt for weapons. How would his skilled opponent kill him? Suddenly, a sharpened stick found its way into Menseratis' hands.

It was so small and feeble, Carter stared at it as he marched forward. Menseratis twirled the little stick in his fingers, then brought it swiftly to his lips.

Before Carter could process what was happening, he felt a little prick on his neck. He stopped. Swayed with sudden disorientation, he dropped to his knees. His fingers went to his neck and pulled out a little dart, the same kind of stinger dart that had stuck Nikolai.

Menseratis came down and knelt before him. Carter looked at the man, then back at the dart, but his head was spinning, eyes dizzy. A tiredness poured through his mind like a thick liquid.

"I stole it from a tree, and tipped it with my own concoction of poisons from the plants around us. It is the most gentle way to die. As a man of my word, you will go quietly into the forever dark. No more pain. No more fighting."

Carter's vision became splotched with dark circles. He tried to mouth one final message to his opponent. A statement of gratitude, but found himself incapable of forming words. If Han was going to die, as Carter almost certainly knew he would, he felt relief in knowing it would be in such a way as this.

Menseratis' face disappeared from sight, his last look one of kindness.

"Go in peace," came the alien's words, cutting through the increasing darkness.

Peace, thought Carter. As the world around him faded, he beheld Taliah's eyes briefly; it was the last thing he saw before death seized him.

CHAPTER 22

"When did they capture her?" Zoar-Wrel asked from the view screen. "If she talks, it will be the end for us all."

Her proclamation of doom didn't go unnoticed by Telmar. Since he heard the terrible news himself from one of his operatives aboard the observer ship, he felt the same way. How long could Taliah hold out against the torture being inflicted on her before she broke down?

"Not long after the arena match began."

His answer appeared to pacify her, at least a little. "Then time may still be on our side. If I know anything about my Overlord counterparts, they will not use the worms against her until they've exhausted all other forms of persuasion."

Telmar put his hand to his stubbled chin and rubbed it. "Time or not, Taliah's up there, facing who knows what. We have to get her out before it's too late."

If Overlords could growl, Telmar was certain she would now. "What do you suggest? If we launched a rescue mission, they'd see it in an instant. Sulit-Bay would kill Taliah out of spite, just so we wouldn't get our hands on her."

He had wrestled with the same question himself. How could they get her out without being seen?

Narrow at first, Zoar-Wrel's slitted eyes widened with an idea. "You mentioned an operative on board the observer ship. Is he in a position to do something?"

"Not rescue her, if that's what you mean. He works in maintenance, mostly in the lower levels. No reason for him to be on the top deck, let alone the interrogation room. We're fortunate he discovered what had happened to Taliah when he did."

The two stared at one another, Telmar hoping the Overlord had a solution, and she probably the same thing. The long silence made it apparent that Zoar-Wrel believed Taliah had no chance. But before the end came for her, she'd tell Sulit-Bay everything she knew about the rebellion. All those ships and troops poised to attack, only to be betrayed by one of their own. How do you make amends to the dead for their empty sacrifice? Sacrifice. He had resisted going in that direction, but given their dire situation, they no longer had the luxury of taking the moral high ground.

"That ship is in a fixed position above the arena, is it not?" he asked.

"Yes. Of course."

"An easy target for a focused proton beam. I estimate a three-second burst would do its work."

The reaction offered by Zoar-Wrel said what words could not. "Are you suggesting what I think you're suggesting?"

"We bring down the ship."

"Killing everyone on board, including Taliah. Your friend and fellow Axanarian."

The realization of what he suggested filled his heart with blackness. He couldn't believe he had even brought up such a thing, the cost to him was more than he could ever estimate. "Yes."

"In the history of your people, there has never been a single instance when one of your kind has ever killed another with deliberate intent. Your most sacred laws declare you will face the same punishment both in this life and the next. Is that what you're advocating?"

It was, as much as he feared the consequences of his actions.

Zoar-Wrel shook her head. "No. There must be another way. Something we've overlooked."

"If we have, then now's the time to bring it up. I feel like I'm a blind man stumbling in the dark, with no way out."

The last part of what he said registered on the Overlord's face. "Blind. You said blind."

What did that have to do with anything? "Yes. What of it?"

She folded her arms together and dropped her gaze, as though thinking deeply about something. "Blind," she repeated several times. All at once, her face lit with recognition. "I have it."

Telmar's hopes buoyed within him. Any other suggestion had to be better than his. The only question for him rested on the singular issue of Taliah's safe return.

"If you've got an idea, now's the time to speak it."

"Not a focused proton beam, but a communications overload. Feed too much information into the incoming data stream, and the operational systems will shut down until they can be reset. During that time, the observer ship will be deaf, dumb, and blind."

Of course. The idea was brilliant, yet so simple. The only thing he didn't like about it was that he didn't come up with the idea. At least one of them did.

"That should be a simple matter," Telmar said. "I can have my contact configure a simple program that will increase the signal bandwidth by a factor of a hundred. No one will know what's happening. In the midst of all the chaos, we send up a ship to rescue her."

"I'll make sure a shuttle will be waiting for you in the central starport with your team."

The plan was still risky, but with the time constraints they faced, they had no other choice. "I'll take care of the arrangements myself, only, it will be a team of one."

She didn't like that idea, or so her contorted face suggested. "One? Just one? Are you being a little cavalier about this? The observer ship may be out of commission for a short while, but they still have guards posted on every deck. How far could you go on your own?"

"Farther than with a dozen boarders creating a commotion. No. Stealth in this instance is the best approach. We also don't have the luxury of time, since it will take time to put a team together. Every second we delay means Taliah is that much closer to breaking."

"I suppose you're right." Zoar-Wrel drew in a quick breath. "The ship you need will be ready by the time you arrive at the starport. Good luck." The screen went dark.

Luck. He would need all there was.

* * *

Telmar hovered above a rocky outcropping outside the arena and waited. The controls in his hands responded to the slightest touch. Up, down, left or right. Whichever way he desired, the shuttle followed his commands without the least little hesitation. Fortunately for him, the approach from the starport had been masked by a combination of high mountains and deep channels cut into the surface of the planet. If he had miscalculated, and was picked up by the observer ship's scanners, he'd already be dead.

On the other side of the arena walls, the three humans fought for their lives against Menseratis. He already knew Carter Stone's fate. The success of the uprising depended on it. But what of his two companions? Did they have a chance against an opponent who had cheated death time and again?

An interesting question, but irrelevant. He had come to rescue Taliah. Not speculate about a combatant's fighting skills.

The longer he waited, the more his hands grew clammy wrapped tight around the control sticks. What was taking so long? His contact aboard the observer ship had assured him he could overload the data systems in short order. So far, that promise had been an empty one.

It also presumed his contact was still in a position to overload the systems. What if he had been caught? Or worse yet, not a contact at all, but a spy loyal to the Raxion Union. If the whole thing had in reality been a setup, he was indeed dead.

As Telmar fidgeted with the controls, he considered what his best escape route might be if the ship hovering above started firing on him. His chances of escape were dismal at best, but at least he'd go down fighting.

Several more minutes went by, and still no signal. How long could Taliah hold out? Perhaps she had already broken, and counter-measures were already being implemented against those who yearned for freedom.

A soft ping sounded in the cabin.

Telmar looked down at the central display. The streams of data coming and going from the ship grew in intensity by about a hundred fold, just the way he had planned. All at once, it dropped off to zero. This was the moment he had been waiting for.

Moving the control sticks upward, the shuttle rose straight up into the air. Several quick course corrections put him on a direct course for the observer ship. Because of his relative position to it, he reached the underside in less than a minute. Moving toward the aft section of the ship, he came out from underneath it and elevated the shuttle to roughly the same altitude as the top deck. Without any portholes or other observation venues in that part of the ship, he could maneuver without being seen. Of course, it also depended on how long communications were knocked out of commission. Only minutes by his estimation. He needed to move fast.

With a gentle nudge forward the shuttle moved along the length of the hull. There in front of him was the emergency hatch. It had the good fortune of being on the top deck where they most likely kept Taliah, but at the same time, down from the main control room where a majority of the crew operated the ship.

Knowing time was slipping by, he set the shuttle down in front of the hatch. He unlatched his restraints and climbed out of the pilot's chair. When Telmar waved his hand over the sensor, the side door retracted after a sharp bang. He peered outside, making sure no guards patrolled the outer part of the ship. When he didn't see any, Telmar went to the hatch and opened it. A blast of cold air hit him when he did.

Gentle hums of varying range emanated from the deck plates underneath Telmar's feet. No doubt power conduits that ran through the ship. He moved forward like a creature of stealth. So far, nothing. Not even a pair of crew members engaged in conversation. Strange. With the ship's communication systems neutralized, he figured there'd be technicians checking relays and support systems in an effort to figure out what had happened.

Perhaps they did, and were waiting for him to make his rescue. Telmar wiped away a light sheen of perspiration from his forehead.

At the end of the narrow corridor, he came across another door. Unlike the emergency hatch, this one had a window. He came in low so as to keep from being seen. Rising up slowly, he viewed the ship's command center. Several techs stood at their stations, inputting commands and responding to orders given by someone he couldn't see. Sulit-Bay perhaps?

Wait. If he had reached the command center, he had gone too far. The interrogation room should be a few doors back off the main corridor. He spun around and went back in the direction he had come. One door after another passed by, until he reached one without any markings.

"This must be it," he said to himself.

If only it had a window like the one that granted him access into the command center. Then he could see if anyone was in the room with Taliah, assuming she was still alive.

His fingers found the access plate, and pressed it. The door slid open with a silent swoosh. Without hesitation, Telmar jumped inside. Strapped down on a table in front of him lay Taliah, not moving. He studied her a second, hoping for any sign of life.

One of her fingers twitched, and her head moved slightly. Feeling the weight of the world lift from his shoulders, he rushed to her side.

"Taliah. Are you okay?" He stroked her matted hair. "Can you hear me?"

Her eyes opened, but just barely. A word formed on her lips, but nothing came out.

"Don't speak. I'm here to get you off this ship."

"What are you doing in here?!" a voice barked from behind.

Telmar tensed. He had the foresight to bring a weapon, but he didn't want to use it just yet. One unintended blast, and the entire crew would be on him in seconds.

His open hands held outward, he slowly turned around.

In the doorway, a guard pointed a plasma gun at him. "I asked you a question. What are you doing in here? This room is restricted."

Thinking fast, Telmar flicked a glance in Taliah's direction. "I was sent by first tier Sulit-Bay. He wanted her watched in case she decided to cooperate."

The guard looked at Taliah, then back at Telmar. The way he nervously held his weapon let Telmar know he was scared under his confident exterior. Information Telmar could use.

"I have my orders." His voice wavered on the last word. "No one in this room without the expressed permission of the first tier."

"I'm giving you new orders." Telmar stood erect, hoping his show of bravado would intimidate the guard.

"What's your name and identification number? I'll have to confirm this."

Telmar played it casual and gave the guard a fake ID badge.

As the guard turned toward the com panel, Telmar swung his leg sideways, striking the guard's chest. He staggered back, and slammed his head into the wall, knocking him out. He fell onto the deck in a crumpled heap.

Fearing he might have been heard, Telmar checked the corridor. Other than the constant hum, nothing.

Exhaling a quick breath, he spun around and took off the

restraints holding Taliah down.

With a gentle heave, he lifted her into his arms and made his way toward the door. Just one thing remained before he left.

Inside his pocket, a small explosive device. Set for the highest yield, he slapped the metallic cylinder against the wall, then made his way back to the shuttle. With each step, Taliah roused further into consciousness.

"What are you doing?" she murmured, as though in a light sleep. "The silver thing. Against the wall. Why?"

"A bomb," he replied tersely. "To mask our escape. If they think you're dead, they won't be looking for you."

Telmar bent down low and stepped through the emergency hatch. To his relief, the shuttle was still there, waiting for him. He set her inside the cabin, then jumped into the pilot's chair. Counting down the seconds in his head, he knew the device would go off at any moment.

Powering up the shuttle's engines, it lifted off the deck and pulled away from the observer ship. All at once, a strong explosion rocked his nimble craft. The blast wave slammed into the hull, sending his ship downward. Proximity alarms rang out as he headed straight for the arena below.

"Hang on," he shouted, and pulled the directional sticks back with all his might.

The shuttle reacted in an instant, and darted up just as they were about to slam into the side of the structure. A grove of yellow trees passed by harmlessly underneath until they fell out of sight.

He reached behind and took hold of Taliah's hand. His heart leapt when she squeezed it tight.

"I got you," he said, "and I'm never letting go."

CHAPTER 23

Menseratis stood over Carter's, Nikolai's, and Han's lifeless bodies lined up on the ground before him.

A prominent hole on one side of the observer ship, it had descended into an open area of the arena at his appearance from the jungle. It had been the same for him from the first match. Bring out his victims, line them up side-by-side on the ground like trophies, and then thrust his hand into the air as a signal of triumph against his enemies. And every time in response, the observer ship landed on the ground, and the first tier came out and congratulated him for his cunning skills and ultimate victory.

This time had been no exception, only, there had been a significant difference. The unexplained explosion several hours before. A flash of light caught his attention as he tracked Han's movements, followed by a blast wave that shook the trees. But there couldn't have been too much damage to the ship, or it would have been brought down.

The side panel opened, and out came a dozen guards armed with pain sticks. They fanned out around Menseratis, their weapons at the ready. Only after the area had been secured did Sulit-Bay appear, Telmin-Kai at his side, like always. The second tier Overlord often reminded him of a Denebian puppy seal, which often struggled to keep up with its mother as it hunted for food, the sight of which being both humorous and sad.

"Congratulations on another hard fought victory," Sulit-Bay applauded him. "Most impressive."

Gratified by the compliment given him, Menseratis offered the Overlord a slight bow in response. "Thank you."

Sulit-Bay examined the bodies like a shopper in the market assaying the quality of merchandise before him. Both Nikolai and Han were covered in blood, an obvious indicator of how they met their death. As he peered close, the Overlord took particular notice of the injuries that riddled their bodies.

"Puncture wounds," Menseratis said. "The bamboo in this arena made for most effective weapons."

"As noted in my initial report."

The Overlord's attention drifted in Carter's direction. Of the three, his body stood out from the others. Other than his pale skin and faraway expression, he didn't have a mark on him. It was as though he dropped dead for no reason.

"This person, Carter Stone," Telmin-Kai said. "He's a strange one."

Menseratis paid the Overlord little mind. He couldn't say why, but there was something about him in particular that especially grated on his nerves. Was it his general appearance that rankled him, or his scheming nature? Menseratis understood his kind all too well. Loyal and deferential to authority on the outside. Inside, he bided his time until an opportunity for advancement presented itself, then pounced on it. Didn't matter if he was deserving of the promotion given him, so long as he got it.

"In what way?"

Only when Menseratis tipped his head in Telmin-Kai's direction—he figured it might be best if he displayed a certain measure of submissiveness himself—did he notice the Overlord's arm was in a sling. And the way he stood also didn't go unnoticed by him. Not erect, his weight evenly distributed on both feet the way Overlords normally stood, but at an angle, as though he favored one side of his body over the other. Then it occurred to him why. The explosion. He must have been injured in the blast. Menseratis took small comfort in the idea that the Overlords were not super beings. They could be injured, which meant they could be killed.

"You were there. Did you not think it odd he came at you in the open? No cover from the jungle. No use of subterfuge. It was as though he wanted to die, and quickly."

"He was a brave man," Menseratis replied. "Few combatants in these arena matches possessed the courage he did."

Telmin-Kai looked at him strangely. "Respect for an opponent you defeated? That is unprecedented. The victors are usually happy to have survived the match, or brayed in triumph after their victory, much like you do. But respect for the fallen, that is a response I have not observed in a long time."

Menseratis didn't care what the Overlord thought. If permitted, he'd be happy to fight against him. One on one. No weapons. Just the cunning of two warriors fighting to the death. If it meant one less Overlord in the universe, even at his own peril, then it would be worth it.

"There is such a thing as honor in defeat. This one didn't play any games. It was just him and me, and I defeated him."

"With a bit of deceit on your part, I might add," Sulit-Bay commented. He bent down and examined Carter's neck. His lips bent into a smile of satisfaction. "I must admit, I didn't expect your use of a stinger dart. He never knew what hit him. Also noted in my preliminary report."

"It was at least a merciful death, unlike the others."

Menseratis' words registered in Telmin-Kai's eyes. The muscles in his face grew taught; his gaze bore down on the damaged ship. "More than what that traitor deserved."

An effective tool in any fight was giving the enemy the impression you were weaker than you actually were. When an opponent thought that, he often dropped his guard and didn't take the required precautions needed to win. That's when Menseratis would spring his trap, and strike when his enemy least expected it. In this case, playing dumb. The dumber they thought you were, the more they revealed.

"Oh? Who is it who dared defy the Raxion Union?"

Telmin-Kai spat on the ground near the three bodies. "Their trainer. Taliah of Axinar IV."

Menseratis put his hand to his chin, hoping it would convey the idea he wasn't quite sure who she was. "I have a vague notion about her. She must have done her job well. Otherwise, they wouldn't have reached their fifth match, with three combatants, no less."

"A skilled fighter. Yes." Telmin-Kai rubbed his injured shoulder. A muted grimace flashed across his face when he did. "As for her allegiances, she picked the wrong side."

"When you say 'picked,' that implies an action from the past, as though she's no longer with us." Menseratis knew exactly what the Overlord meant, but kept up his façade. "Dead. She's dead, isn't she?"

"Killed by her own people, at least that's what our initial investigation indicates."

"That doesn't make any sense. Why would they eliminate one of their own?" On that point, Menseratis was truly in the dark.

"Now that her team has been eliminated, it doesn't matter much anymore." Sulit-Bay's eyes combed over the three bodies before him.

Now Menseratis felt truly lost.

Sulit-Bay must have picked up on his confusion. He patted his subordinate's good shoulder as a show of empathy, which surprised him. Overlords, as a species with position in the empire, never acted demonstrably with one another. They thought it unseemly. "Don't mind him too much. The explosion that killed Taliah injured a number of the crew, including my second here. I think he's letting his anger speak for him."

Now it all made sense. Somehow, Taliah's compatriots planted a bomb on the observer ship, and she was killed in the blast. Two questions. Why was she there, and why were her supposed friends so intent on eliminating her? Did it have to do with the planned insurrection against the Raxion Union?

"The only thing I can surmise," Menseratis concluded, "was that the assassin or assassins feared what she had to say, and so they silenced her."

A note of congratulations flickered in Sulit-Bay's slitted eyes. "Very good. It's that kind of deductive reasoning that propelled you to the final arena match." He clasped his hands behind his back and stood a little taller. "Yes, we had our suspicions about her loyalty to the Empire. When one doesn't have the proper answers, questions are asked. It seems those she protected feared what she had to say, and killed her before she could betray them."

"I assume you will search for those misguided fools."

"Of course. They may have employed a clever tactic to get the saboteurs on board to carry out the deed, but that doesn't mean they left without leaving evidence behind. We will track them down soon enough."

Of that, Menseratis had no doubt. "I pray you find every success against your enemies."

"Speaking of enemies," Telmin-Kai said, "there is one thing that did perplex me during your last match."

Menseratis couldn't imagine what that would be. He fought and defeated his three opponents. Why would that vex him? "My apologies. Ask, and I will answer to the best of my ability."

The first tier knelt beside the three bodies and studied them close. "This one," he said as he pointed at Han. "You said you killed him with a bamboo spear."

"Yes."

"Other than the blood and wounds we see, there is no record of the fight. Nothing."

A burst of laughter preceded Menseratis' response. "A simple explanation." He likewise pointed at Han. "Of the three, this one was the most cunning, and unpredictable. I know the purpose of these matches is the study of our fighting skills and tactics. I count it a great honor to aid in the greatness of your empire. However, a fight in the open, or at least visible enough from your ship above, put me at a great disadvantage against his skills. He blended in with his surroundings so effectively, it was like he became a part of the jungle. So I employed the same strategy as this gallant fighter, and caught him unaware in the marsh pit, which is, as you know, in the densest part of the jungle. I think the results speak for themselves."

Sulit-Bay gave Han's limp body a shove with his foot. "Most impressive."

The action sparked a thought in Menseratis. His victory clearly established, an important task awaited him, and every moment he delayed put it in jeopardy. He assumed a posture of respect as he faced both Overlords. "I indulge your understand-ing, but there is a ceremony that must be performed, and time is of the essence. If I have found favor in your sight, it is my hope you grant my request."

The words sounded clunky and forced in Menseratis' ears, as it did Sulit-Bay's. His cheerful disposition turned at the word 'indulge,' and darkened as the seconds passed.

"What kind of ceremony?" the first tier Overlord asked.

"It is difficult to explain. Picture in your mind a wayfarer who has been charged with a great responsibility. It is a prayer that must be said over these men so that their essences will find rest in the world to come."

Sulit-Bay and Telmin-Kai looked at one another before they turned back to Menseratis. The expected answer did not come at first. Instead, both Overlords stared at him in harsh silence. He feared he may have overstepped the good wishes previously of-fered him, which shouldn't have been a surprise. No matter how much they may have respected his skills as a fighter, underneath all the accolades offered him, Menseratis was no better than a performing animal in their eyes.

"You may say your prayer," Sulit-Bay finally replied, "though you have never made this request before."

"I have not come across skilled fighters such as these before. They deserve special recognition."

The first tier Overlord took a step back and pointed at the

three. "Then proceed."

"Not here. In the mortuariam, where the dead are brought after each arena match. That is the appropriate place for such a prayer."

Sulit-Bay considered his request before he replied. "A most unusual practice, but because of your extraordinary fighting skills in the arena, I will grant your request."

"Thank you, first tier."

* * *

The shuttle came for the bodies under Menseratis' charge not long after Telmin-Kai contacted the central starport. The flight techs adhered to his wishes, and treated the three fallen fighters with great respect, which stood in stark contrast with the way they normally disposed of the fallen.

Two techs per body, they placed Carter, Nikolai, and Han on an anti-grav table brought with them on the shuttle and maneuvered the three into the mortuariam's exam room after the ship landed. Unlike the planet's surface, this place was cold, and sterile. A tile-like material covered the floors and walls. Above, bright lights bathed the room in white, which gave it an ethereal quality.

The techs lifted each man and placed him on a metallic table in the middle of the room, again, with great care.

Menseratis stood before the three and clasped his hands together with his head bowed. Both eyes closed tight, he silently mouthed the prayer. As he spoke them in his mind, he became acutely aware of six pairs of eyes on him. He turned around and faced the techs. "What must be said must be said in private. I do not think you wish a bad report be made regarding your treatment of this most somber of ceremonies."

Spoken with the brunt force of an Overlord, Menseratis made his wishes quite clear. Force was the language their people understood and respected, even when it came from a subjugated species.

Without a word, the six techs left the mortuariam, not one of them offering the slightest objection at being treated in such a way by someone they considered an inferior. Only after the door closed behind them did Menseratis fix his attention on Han. An air of anticipation descended on him. Since his arrival in the clearing with the three at the end of the match, he counted off the time in his head. If he figured it right, he should—

Han suddenly bolted up, a look of terror cut into his face. His eyes darted back and forth as he drew in several frantic breaths. "Where am I?"

"Someplace safe."

CHAPTER 24

Han stared at the sterile room around him. Slowly, his awareness sharpened as his senses returned.

His plan had worked.

Back in the arena, as Menseratis hunted him, an idea had formed in his mind. It felt incredibly risky, but Han suffered no delusion regarding his chances against his opponent. Gaining an audience with his enemy, under the thickest part of the jungle arena, out of sight from the observers above was his only chance. And he'd pulled it off. Menseratis, he discovered, was not the heartless killer they'd imagined. When he talked with him, he felt a kinship. It solidified his hope that he just might acquire his opponent's aid. And when Han laid out why Carter had been so willing to get himself killed, Menseratis grew intrigued. Han told him all that he knew, and he eagerly offered his help. Clearly, Menseratis hated the Overlords and these killing arenas just as much as his own team had.

And now they were...

Han found Menseratis' eyes as he stood, arms folded by the bodies of Carter and Nikolai.

"Are we at the morgue?"

"Yes, though it's actually referred to as a mortuariam," Menseratis corrected him. "How are you feeling? The poison I used to kill Carter is the same I used on you, only half the strength. It put you in what we call on my world a sleep death. Do you ache anywhere?"

Han breathed in, and reassessed his body. "Actually, I feel very good. Rested."

Menseratis smiled. "That is a common result for this particular family of toxins. A feeling of having slept for an extended period of time."

The door to the morgue opened. And in stepped an Overlord, alone. Han stared at the intruder's face, his hands clasped into fists. Was this the ally he was told to expect, or someone else? He'd never met any of the Overlords who were involved in the rebellion. He noted the same concerned look on Menseratis. If it wasn't, and they had been discovered, this place would indeed serve as a morgue.

The Overlord stepped into the room and studied them with great interest before she shut the door.

"I am Ywen-On," said the Overlord. "Who are you two?" Her voice bore a trace of menace, or was it concern?

"Are you here for... Carter?" asked Han cryptically.

Ywen-On nodded. "Yes. I am," she replied.

Han felt immense relief, and let out a heavy breath. This Overlord was an ally.

"I am Carter's teammate, and this," he gestured to his former enemy. "This is Menseratis. He has asked to help us."

A look that Han had never seen on an Overlord washed across Ywen-On's face. The closest he could describe it was uncertainty, perhaps even confusion. Of the Overlords he had met, they always knew exactly what they wanted. "I don't understand how you two are here right now."

"It is a long story," said Han. "One to be told after we bring down the Raxion Union this day."

A smile formed on the Overlord's face. She hurried over to Carter.

"This won't take long."

* * *

Carter felt something. It was the strangest thing. To feel. A tingling warmth spread through his body.

Voices began tumbling into his mind from outside.

Can Nikolai be revived too?

I am afraid not. His wounds are too extensive.

How is Carter doing?

He's waking.

Will he fully recover?

It's hard to say.

Carter tried to initiate some form of movement. His fingers. It was a strange sensation, trying to figure out how to move them. Trying to reconnect his brain to place where they were on his body.

Did you see that? I thought I saw his fingers twitch.

He's beginning to wake. It will take some time.

Can he hear us?

If he is moving his fingers, then yes. Auditory functions are the first to return.

Carter lay still for a time, soaking up the feel of life returning to his body.

Have you removed the devices from his head?

Yes, they're out. No one can hear anything, not that they'd be listening anymore. They think he's dead now. But just to be sure, I disposed of them. The listening device, and his tracker. To us Overlords, he's now non-existent.

Where is Taliah? I thought she'd be here.

Carter felt his heart leap at her name. Her plan had worked! She would be immensely relieved. He remembered their moment together as he pledged his agreement to her plan. She had been in tears, and he had held her.

We don't know Taliah's fate. She was caught by Sulit-Bay and Telmin-Kai. They were interrogating her.

Then security forces could be upon us at any moment.

Not likely. We rescued her before they used the bore worms. However, we don't know where she and our operative, Telmar, have gone. They've fallen off the grid.

Carter squeezed his fists. Tried to lift himself up, but his head fell back against the bed.

"He's waking!" said Han's jubilant voice.

One thing Carter knew was this. He wanted to see Taliah's face again. His heart burned even now, as he imagined her in some peril. Running for her life.

Carter opened his eyes. Through blurred vision he saw Han's face. A smile appeared instantly. There was also the familiar face of Ywen-On. And then a third face appeared. A face that gave Carter a surge of energy that jolted him up in bed.

"Menseratis?!"

* * *

Taliah ducked low beneath the large fronds of a thick bushy

tree. Overhead, the mechanical whine of a search pod raced overhead.

Those little things were everywhere.

She and Telmar had fled their little craft as soon as it landed. And now the jungle was crawling with searchers.

"Come on!" said Taliah, grabbing Telmar's hand as she motioned toward an open stretch.

They were not far from the arena where her fighters were still presumably entrenched in battle. If she knew Carter as well as she thought she did, he'd stay alive as long as possible, which would give the insurgents the time needed to position themselves before Zoar-Wrel gave the attack order. If he died too soon, it could cost many thousands of lives. Of course, he didn't go in alone. Nikolai and Han were valiant warriors. When Carter went down, they'd still give Menseratis a fight. If she were honest with herself, they had no chance against him. His regenerative abilities coupled with his advanced fighting skills were most likely too much for the Earthers. Could the match already be decided? A quick look upward as they went around a large baobab tree produced an empty sky. No observer ship. It could have positioned itself on the opposite side of the arena, out of site, but more likely, landed to congratulate the winner, most likely, Menseratis.

These thoughts plagued her even as she and Telmar ran for their lives.

She had one goal. Get to the mortuariam. No one would expect her there, and she could hide in relative safety until they brought Carter's body.

The mortuariam's roof jutted above the trees. To their left lay the Positron Center, towering nine levels over the jungle floor. They had passed it safely enough. Soon, she hoped to see Carter brought to life there, if Ywen-On hadn't yet been discovered. Sulit-Bay had sniffer drones everywhere.

Taliah gripped Telmar's hand tight as she led them into the side opening.

She suddenly froze. Standing inside the doorway was Telmin-Kai, flanked by two Overlord soldiers.

The look on Telmin-Kai's face when he saw her was one of supreme surprise.

Beside her, Telmar drew his gun.

She barely had time to dive to the ground before the sound of weapon discharges tore through the air.

* * *

Zoar-Wrel paced nervously as she waited within the Positron Center. She noted the lights on her communication consul. All the rebel ships waited for her command. She imagined them in her mind. Hundreds upon hundreds of war vessels across so many worlds. Hiding in gaseous anomalies, behind collapsed stars, all in anticipation of her signal.

A chime sounded from the consul; the noise jolted her like electricity.

She raced over to the communicator.

"This is the Mother controller, we are in quiet mode. Do you copy?"

"I am sorry, Mother, but I detect large movements of ships. The... intruders are scouring our home for the children."

She understood the coded words perfectly. The Overlords had gone on high alert. Something must have happened that triggered this response. Did they catch Taliah? Did they force her to talk?

Another chime sounded. This one from a world called Tarmox Prime.

"This is the Mother controller—"

"Mother, some of our children are coming under attack from the intruders. Please advise. Is hope near?"

Zoar-Wrel's mind raced. The plan was falling apart before it had been initiated. Her cursed Raxion Union had sniffed enough out, and they were no longer content to hide and gather information. They were beginning to go on the hunt.

Another chime sounded from the communicator. Then a fourth. A fifth. Soon, too many to answer.

Amidst the sounds, a noise from Zoar-Wrel's belt cut through the clamor. It was Ywen-On.

"Ywen-On!" growled Zoar-Wrel in desperation. "The resistance ships are beginning to fall under attack."

"Tell them to hold steady!" came Ywen-On's shaking voice. "Carter has been revived. He's heading to your location now. Tell the leaders to hold on to Hope. Victory is on the way."

CHAPTER 25

Carter hurried out of the mortuariam, Han and Menseratis following close behind. Carter was the only one with a firearm, given him by Ywen-On, but Han and Menseratis had picked up surgical knives as weapons.

"What is the plan?" asked Menseratis.

It surprised Carter just how quickly his mind focused after his brush with death. Since he awakened he had just one thought—shut down the power.

A clear path lay between him and his objective. All he had to do was meet up with Zoar-Wrel, and follow her instructions. Ywen-On had given him specific details about how to reach her and handed him a schematic map, just in case he needed it.

"You and Han can help ensure I reach the Positron Center in one piece. Once I'm safely inside, everything will rest on me."

The sudden sound of weapons fire halted Carter. He looked at Han, as if he might have an answer, but his friend only shook his head.

"It's coming from over there," said Menseratis. "Close to the Positron Center."

"It appears I might need both of you after all."

* * *

It had all happened so fast, Taliah barely had a chance to look up from where she'd flung herself. One of the Overlord guards lay on its back, dead. Telmin-Kai and the other guard looked at her, as if she were a lost gem they had just recovered. And that meant...

She looked over at her fellow Axinarian. Telmar crouched down on the ground, face towards her. His eyes almost met hers, only, it was as if they were looking just above her. And their still-ness told her everything. Her friend was gone.

"Clever girl," said the second tier Overlord. "We thought you were dead."

Taliah looked up at Telmin-Kai, who had moved closer to her. The guard pointed the weapon in her direction.

"You should know the good news," said Telmin-Kai. "We've already begun rooting out your resistance forces. We grew tired of waiting. So far, I am told we've found a number of contraband ships in hiding. And with your help, we'll find the rest. Well, not entirely all your help. The bore worms will loosen your tongue soon enough."

She stood shakily. She couldn't let them take her alive.

"Stun her!" said Telmin-Kai quickly

The guard raised his gun, but never fired.

A blast sounded from the jungle close by, and the guard dropped dead.

Stepping out from the foliage was Carter and two other fig-ures that Taliah couldn't believe were there. It was a miracle. Her heart pounded as her and Carter's eyes met.

She glanced quickly up at Telmin-Kai. The look on his face

was that of an Overlord who'd just seen a three-headed Draco-
sian cave worf.

Taliah sprang to her feet as Carter rushed to her side. She
closed the distance and swallowed Carter in her arms. "You're
alive!"

Carter's smile grew big, and she drank it in as he looked deep
into her eyes. She felt his relief in finding her. Felt... his affection.

"There is a saying where I come from," said Han. "Man who
stares too long at girl gets ants in pants."

Carter kept his eyes on her. "You looked surprised to see
me. Your plan has worked beautifully."

Taliah smiled. Then it was as if her senses caught up to her
after being entranced by the man holding her in his arms. She
stepped back and appraised Han, and then the other man she
hadn't noticed... it wasn't Nikolai. It was... Menseratis?!

"What's going on? How did Han and Menseratis both make
it out of the arena?!"

"That's what I want to know," Telmin-Kai demanded, his
face marked by a sneer.

Menseratis stood holding both of the dead guards' weapons.
He tossed one to Han. "I poisoned Carter and Han. Carter I
killed, Han I put into a coma." Menseratis stepped close to
Telmin-Kai, and the Overlord shuddered at his proximity and
sounded his fear with a squeaking noise. Taliah had only heard it
a few times, when an Overlord underling was about to receive a
beating. It was their version of a whimper.

"You think you are so superior to all of us," said Menseratis.
"You'll never be superior. You're nothing more than cruel and
heartless monsters. Creatures like that will always be inferior,
even if they were to rule the entire galaxy." Menseratis pointed at

Taliah and Carter. "Did you see the way they ran to each other—
the way they held each other? What you saw is more powerful
than all the weapon power in your entire Raxion arsenal. That!
Love and heart and passion. That is what will bring your empire
crashing down around you. Every revolutionary working against
you now is propelled by that same heart. A passion to see their
people free."

Carter stepped up to Telmin-Kai. "I was a cold-blooded killer
back on my home world. If I was the same person now as I was
then, I'd have no qualm shooting you in the head this very moment, but I've changed. What Menseratis said is true. Your people are heartless monsters who hurt good people and destroy
lives, and all for what? To keep your pathetic race in power. But
I've found a better way." He turned to Taliah. "I've got to complete the mission. I'll leave you in Menseratis' capable care."

"Be careful, Carter," said Taliah. "No more dying, okay?"

She smiled warmly at him and he nodded.

Without another word, Carter and Han ran toward the Positron Center.

Menseratis tied Telmin-Kai's wrists in one of the guard's
hand locks. Satisfied it would hold him tight, he struck the Overlord in the face, knocking him out.

"There will be more out looking for us soon," said Taliah.
"We should find a place to hide."

Menseratis faced the jungle. "Follow me. I know a thing or
two about hiding."

* * *

Zoar-Wrel shouted into the command console, "All fighters,
rendezvous at your appointed coordinates. Take out any soft

targets and wait for my command to engage the main Raxion fleets."

She'd dropped the covert language. It was unnecessary now that the fighting had started, and her signal was being tracked. She watched as her carefully designed safeguards and traps begin to fall as a team of her own people began tearing them down to discover her location.

Soon, the Positron Center would be crawling with Overlord soldiers.

Where was Carter? If anything happened to him, all would be lost.

"Come on, Carter," she said to herself. "Don't let me down."

An idea came to mind. She didn't know what the security forces were doing presently, but perhaps the Center had received an influx of guards. That would make it difficult for Carter to enter.

She turned again to the command console. "Mother needs assistance. All children nearby, rendezvous at Mother's home planet. Please clear a path around her castle walls. Repeat, please clear a path around Mother's walls."

Zoar-Wrel held her breath. All she could do was wait and watch her security traps continue to fall one-by-one.

Carter. Where are you? You haven't much time.

* * *

"Helmet!" barked Sulit-Bay.

An Overlord flight assistant quickly fit a large red helmet onto Sulit-Bay's head.

Another Overlord frowned from the tarmac below Sulit-Bay's

sleek Xios shuttle. It was a nimble craft packed with the powerful energy blasters that all the Raxion carried. But this was his personal shuttle, and so he had retrofitted it with a nasty assortment of additional weapons. He already had one particular one in mind that he hoped to use.

Sulit-Bay glared down at the Overlord staring unhappily up at him. His name was Geel-Sar, one of the High Magistrate's top generals.

"How can you command the fleet when you're fighting yourself?" growled Geel-Sar. "It would be more prudent if you came to the command station and led our armies from there."

"I can lead them fine from here. I prefer to be where the blood is. If I am not in the midst of action, then I am blind."

Sulit-Bay closed the hatch to his shuttle after his personal bodyguards boarded, started the powerful neutron engine, yanked the control lever down, sending him soaring into the sky. Before he could join the fleet assembling to crush the local uprising on the Arena Planet's moon, he had one objective to complete first.

Kill Taliah.

She had escaped him, bringing shame and embarrassment upon his name. An inferior like her getting away with such an insult was intolerable. Rage filled Sulit-Bay's thoughts. Revenge. Furious revenge! He would see to her death personally, and he had a good idea where she'd be. Telmin-Kai's last transmission was not far from the Positron Center, the Empire's greatest achievement. He would bring her down there, and her dead body would lay prostrate in worship before the power of the Raxion strength. He would use the fire torch affixed to his left wing on Taliah, and the Positron Center would be like a god for her body to burn before, her final resting place an altar, and the incense of her burning would rise in fragrant retribution into the stars where her resistance fighters would be utterly crushed by the Empire's fleet.

She would pay. They all would pay... *dearly.*

* * *

Carter crouched on the lip of the jungle before the massive building of the Positron Center. Ten soldiers stood at the entrance. A frontal assault wouldn't work. Carter scanned the edifice. There were no windows on the first three levels either. No way in other than the door.

Ten guards? That's not what he'd expected. Something had happened. The Overlords must be on alert, and in a defensive posture.

"I see no other way than for me to play as decoy," said Han.

"That's suicide," Carter objected.

"We only live once. Or twice, in your case."

Han's humor in the midst of chaos brought a smile to Carter's lips.

"Even if you managed to draw their attention, they would not all leave the entrance. I'd still be left with a handful of guards."

"At least you'd have a chance," Han replied.

Carter shook his head. "There has to be a better solution. Zoar-Wrel might not know of our dilemma. I wish there was some way to communicate with her."

The thought suddenly struck Carter. What if Zoar-Wrel had been found out? Perhaps she'd been taken captive and the plan uncovered, and that was why so many guards were standing outside the door.

Carter's heart sank. He stared up at the sky above and wondered if there might be a big man upstairs watching him now. All the prayers Clarence had made in that church, had they been part of what yanked at Carter's heart? Was it somehow a divine miracle that happened to him?

He sighed, and quietly asked for another miracle.

A low rumble hummed in the air, faint at first, then grew louder. Carter noticed specks dot the harsh blue sky above, then suddenly the fighters were down firing fiercely all around the Positron Center.

"Amen!" shouted Carter.

"Look!" cried Han. "There's a force shield."

Han was right. The fighters' weapon blasts exploded in thin air above the Positron Center. Clearly, it was the reason why Taliah needed Carter to get inside. All firepower was ineffectual against the Overlords' armaments due to the energy source within the Center.

Carter glanced at the guards surrounding the door. They had positioned themselves in the grass, firing up at the fighters darting through the air.

"They're distracted. This is our chance."

"Your chance," said Han. "This is where we part. You have the tracker removed while I don't. In my economy, that's a liability."

Who could argue with that kind of logic? It had been the plan all along that Carter would enter the Center alone. Undetected. Now that he was about to do it, a feeling of apprehension tugged at his heart. Chances were good they'd never see each other again.

"Right," said Carter. "Take care my friend."

"I will," said Han with a bow of the head and a gleam in his eye. "And... may the force be with you."

Carter shook his head. "Alright, Han Solo."

Springing from the undergrowth, Carter made a straight line to the squad of guards, who were intensely focused on the sky, firing at random at any craft that whizzed by.

Carter's heart raced with anticipation. The main entrance lay ahead of him. A few more steps and—

A high-low bleat of an alarm sounded from the Center. The timing couldn't have been worse. Carter looked over his shoulder. Every head had turned in his direction. Carter spun around and leapt for the doors as energy charges rang out behind him.

Blast after blast struck the ground and walls as he slid through the opening. Each concussion wave slammed into his body, but he couldn't let that keep him from his objective. Keeping down low, he ran down a long hallway towards the T-junction Ywen-On told him about. The first turn was a left.

Carter gripped the gun in his hand and turned over his shoulder and fired. The guards had just entered the building, and his shots caused them to dive for cover as he reached the left turn.

Zoar Wrel was on the fifth floor. Ahead was another right turn. Just as it appeared near the end of the corridor, blasts pounded the wall behind him. He had to get to the carrying pods that would take him to the higher levels. Carter turned and planted his feet. A moment later, two guards rounded the corner and he dropped them both with a pair of shots.

That forced the guards following them to hold back and cautiously look around the corner.

Carter back peddled quickly, holding his gun out, ready to

fire. He'd already killed the Overlord guard who was about to shoot Taliah. He still had his killer instincts, only now, he was using them for good. To cut off the Overlords' brutal grip of power and put an end to slavery and murder on a thousand worlds!

Five more shots rang out from Carter's energy weapon. Another Overlord body dropped. Carter reached the carrying pod that Ywen-On had described and pressed the button. An egg-shaped encasement appeared in the wall. He fired several more shots, then sprang inside.

A keypad glowed above him. The only problem was, the numbers were marked in Overlord symbols. But math was universal, right? He punched the third character. Thank God for logic.

He hadn't gone more than a few dozen meters, when Zoar-Wrel appeared.

Armed with the same logic as before about Raxion symbols, he found the control that stopped the pod, which it did in an instant. When the door opened, he said to the Overlord, "Get in."

CHAPTERS 26

Sulit-Bay's ship swung in low over the jungle. He went faster than his bodyguards behind had anticipated, and they were thrown against the bulkhead before he straightened it out again.

He gripped the directional sticks tighter as his gaze rested on the directional display suspended in front of him. In every direction, plants and trees from a dozen worlds were each analyzed for signs of life bigger than a mole rat. So far, he had come up empty.

"You can't run for long," Sulit-Bay said under his breath.

The more frustrated he became, the closer his ship crept toward the jungle canopy.

"Sir!" a guard called from behind.

The Overlord's head snapped up, just in time to see a mountain ridge coming straight for him.

"Hang on!"

Sulit-Bay jerked the control sticks sideways, banking the shuttle harder than it had been designed. The deck plates ground together under the pressure, moaning like an injured animal in agony. Pops and bangs sounded throughout the ship, so much so, that for a moment, he feared it might break apart.

"Let it break apart," the Overlord growled. The only thing

that mattered was his prey—Taliah. And to a lesser degree, Menseratis. She was a known quantity, whose loyalties were never fully trusted. He knew in his heart she'd betray the Raxion Union the first opportunity she had. It was the way her kind lived. What he didn't expect was the extent of her betrayal. But that would be resolved soon enough.

For Menseratis, he had something special in store for him. The most skilled warrior in a generation had the audacity to be on the cusp of final victory of the arena matches, only to repay the accolades offered him with treachery. That, Sulit-Bay could never forgive, nor would his people ever forget. But first things first.

His ship swung around and hugged the mountain ridge not far from the arena. The two couldn't have gotten too far since their escape. What perplexed Sulit-Bay more was why they hadn't been picked up on the scanners. Their heat signatures should stand out against the rest of the jungle.

"The jungle," the Overlord said aloud. "How can something there not be there?"

"Sir?" one of the guards behind him questioned.

"When it's there but you don't know it," Sulit-Bay answered himself.

"Excuse me, sir," the same guard spoke, this time with greater urgency. "I am receiving a communication from central command. They wish to speak with you about a squadron of Axanarian battle cruisers approaching this planet. All first tiers are ordered to report to the command center."

Sulit-Bay paid him no mind. Instead, he reset the directional display to its lower settings, one that could pick up a microbe on the other side of the planet. The dark green forest suddenly morphed into multiple zones of red and orange. So many, in fact, it looked like the jungle had been bathed in blood. And soon it would be, if Sulit-Bay got his wish.

"Where are you?"

In an open field ahead, the red glow faded into a softer brown. Not surprising, considering not much plant life grew there. Where a couple larger-sized rocks stuck out of the ground, it took on an ochre hue. Then he saw it. A hint of red at the base of it. Something or someone was hiding underneath.

In Sulit-Bay's mind, there could only be one answer what. He moved the control sticks forward, and the ship shot in the direction of the geological form in a burst of acceleration. Nothing else mattered to him except his final act of retribution against two warriors he considered kindred spirits.

Activating his weapons systems, a circular display appeared in the middle of the targeting grid. On his left and right, both ion cannons charged up to full power. These were deaths he would truly enjoy.

As his ship approached, Sulit-Bay sat back in his chair and anticipated just how much he would savor the end of two skilled opponents. His attention drifted upward for just a second, when a figure emerged from behind the rock formation and fired a weapon at the ship.

"Sir!" a guard called out.

But he was too late. The blast struck the aft engine. Multiple alarms rang out as the shuttle pitched onto its side. Sulit-Bay fought for control, but smoke in the cabin made it difficult for him to see. Not certain how much altitude he had lost, the Overlord pulled up, but not enough. The nose struck the ground hard, then tumbled several times, breaking apart as it did, before coming to a stop at the base of a steep cliff.

Sparks popped all around him. Suspended upside down, Su-lit-Bay unstrapped himself, and fell onto the deck. Rather, the roof of his ship. The guards, which had been behind him, lay scattered about, some dead, based on their twisted and mangled forms. The rest, he feared, would soon be dead. Either way, they couldn't help him now.

The Overlord crawled the length of the roof, until a crack in the side showed itself through the smoke. He squeezed through the opening, falling onto the ground not far below. The air was cool compared to the damaged ship's interior. Sulit-Bay drew in several breaths, coughing out the smoke that had settled into his filter gills.

"That's the perfect place for you," a disembodied voice said from out of view. "Rooting around on the ground like a scaven-ger."

Disembodied or not, Sulit-Bay recognized it. "Menseratis." He looked up, and saw him standing not far away, the weapon he presumed took down his ship still in the traitor's hand. Be-side him, Taliah, who appeared content to stay where she was.

"You will look me in the eye when speaking," Sulit-Bay growled.

"Funny. I was thinking the same thing about you."

Sulit-Bay pushed off the ground and rose to his feet. He stood erect, the way all Overlords did in the presence of an infe-rior species. "Surrender now, and it will go well with you, and your people."

The gun in Menseratis' hand rose a little higher. "I am the one with the weapon."

"I'm surprised at you. Hiding behind a firearm. Only cowards threaten this way."

"And you are alone. I could kill you with a twitch of my finger."

The threat did not go unnoticed by Sulit-Bay. "If you plan on killing me, then I suggest you do it now. Otherwise, you let me live, if you don't wish your planet destroyed by a retribution ship."

For the first time, Menseratis' confidence dropped. Not by much, but enough that Sulit-Bay noted it.

"What do you mean?" he asked.

"We first tier Overlords are always connected to one another. That is how the Raxion Union remains strong, always knowing where the other is. And right now, they know where I am. When they come for me, they will find you, and know of your treachery against me. The only payment for such a betrayal is the destruction of your world."

"Only if they find me here."

"And me," Taliah said, jumping in.

A smile of disdain spread across Sulit-Bay's lips. "Such an insipid show of support. It only makes me feel sorrier for you."

"I think you have that in the reverse," Menseratis said.

"What do you mean?" Sulit-Bay asked.

"There is no such connection between your people. If there were, they would have sent a fleet of shuttles by now." His gazed scanned the sky. "Nothing."

Sulit-Bay clasped his hands behind his back. "Let's say you are correct. What do you intend to do? Stand here and talk?"

"Not exactly." He handed his weapon to Taliah, who kept it pointed at him. "We fight."

Perhaps the suns above had baked the fighter's brain. "We

what?"

"You Overlords have put such a premium on personal warfare for generations, and the skills and strategies gleaned from them that kept your empire in power. That stops today. Cut off the head, and the animal dies."

"A quaint notion."

Menseratis rolled up both sleeves halfway up his arm. "I wonder if you have ever tasted the fruit of one-on-one combat for yourself, in front of an enthralled audience no less?" He pointed at Taliah, who nodded in reply.

Was the traitor serious? "You want me to what?"

"As you already know, I have earned the right of the last match." He pointed at the trees that surrounded the clearing. "This will be *our* arena."

"I have no intention of stooping to your level. Only inferiors fight. We Overlords observe and learn."

Taliah fired a shot at Sulit-Bay's feet. "I think you will fight, or I'll kill you myself." She raised the weapon and pointed it at his head.

There had to be a way out of this. Inside his ship, he could send a signal. "Alright. If you insist. But first, let me at least retrieve my battle armor. It will even the odds against a master fighter such as yourself."

A short laugh preceded Menseratis' answer, which surprised Sulit-Bay. Never once had he ever heard someone from his world laugh at anything. "You take me for a fool? There will be no communication transmissions, not until one of us is dead." He took a step back and extended his arms.

Sulit-Bay had no choice. He had to kill him if he had any chance of getting out of this alive. "So be it."

He likewise took a step back and crouched down low.

* * *

Their egg-shaped conveyance came to an abrupt stop.

Zoar-Wrel jumped out when an opening formed. "Hurry," she said. "We don't have much time."

Her statement could not have been more obvious. Of course they needed to hurry. Had she already forgotten about the guards behind them? Carter refrained from a snide remark and kept pace with her.

"How much further?" he asked.

"Not far. At the end of the colonnade."

Her nomenclature for this part of the building was well named. Unlike the other architectural structures he had seen on this planet, it almost felt like a throwback to some forgotten time in the past. Rows of stone columns went by as they ran down the walkway. Above, the ceiling looked like it had been sculpted from a massive piece of rock. In the middle of it, portions had been cut out to let in the suns' light. In other climates, that would have been a problem, what with weather and rain a cyclic issue. On this planet, he never once saw a dark cloud. Only in the arenas did anything appreciable grow, such as the different types of plant life and jungle environments created for various forms of combat. No doubt the result of a sophisticated water system. Outside, in the open plains, a never-ending sweeping desert. Clearly, on this planet, it never rained.

Though he didn't notice at first, Zoar-Wrel's jog slowed. Carter thought she might have been getting tired after a long run, but she seemed as fresh as when they started. Fearing she might have seen something, he pointed his gun in different directions.

"Put that away," she rebuked him. "One misfire, and it will activate the alarm."

"It?" Until then, she hadn't mentioned an it.

"The guard that stands between us and the Positron Center."

One guard almost felt like an insult. More of a joke really. The most important location in the entire empire protected by just one guard. A single blast, and he'd be done away with. "If you have a moral objection about taking a life, it is a qualm for which I have come to respect."

"You don't understand. They're... they're..."

As she struggled for the right word, Carter realized why she couldn't put her thoughts into a tangible form. Standing before a massive metal door was the largest beast he had ever seen. A shadowy creature with six arms and legs stepped into the light. Whatever it was must have been eleven feet high, nine feet wide, and weighed several tons.

The creature raised one of his arms and prevented the two from going past. "What is your business in this area?" it growled in a low, guttural voice.

Carter had to think fast. "Uh..." His mind went blank.

Zoar-Wrel handed the guard a small black card, which he examined closely. "Maintenance check. Some of the outer systems have noted a noticeable degradation of their primary power signals. They've been on back-ups until the problem is resolved. Our orders come from the High Magistrate's inner council."

The card looked miniscule in the behemoth's massive hand. He took it to a device Carter didn't recognize and inserted it into a narrow slot. Already, this was taking longer than he had anticipated. No one said anything about getting past a guard and telling lies about the outer systems. Countless fleets of ships were engaged in the fight for their lives against who knew how many Raxion defenses, both in space and on the ground. The longer it took them to inactivate the core's power outputs, the less likely their chances of success.

"You may proceed," the guard grunted, and then moved aside after he handed Zoar-Wrel her card. The opening he created was just big enough for Carter to slip through. As he hurried down the hallway, he threw a quick glance over his shoulder. To his relief, the guard, monstrosity, whatever that thing was held his spot.

"Man, that was close," he exhaled. "I thought he had us for sure."

A simple nod indicated Zoar-Wrel's thoughts on the matter.

"How did that card you gave him work? There's no degradation in the power signals, is there?"

"I spent half a year creating the code on that card. Does the term hacker have any meaning on your planet?" asked Zoar-Wrel.

"Yes, is that what you are?"

The Overlord chortled lightly. "The best."

When they had gotten within a few feet of the massive door, it slid open in silence, as though carried by air. What Carter saw on the other side literally took his breath away. Bathed in luminous white light, a room the size of a five-story warehouse going back into what seemed like infinity filled his view. Rising up a hundred feet at least, multiple floors filled with thousands of people in front of strange looking terminal outlets stretched into the distance. The sight of it all both enthralled and terrified him.

Zoar-Wrel bent close so only Carter could hear her. "Look

for a unit that is not being used by anyone."

"What are all these people doing here? It's like a city within a city."

"It takes a lot of technicians to run an empire."

Carter made a slow turn so as not to draw attention to himself. They'd be on him in a second if just one tech noticed them.

Over by the wall, he saw dozens of people, some human, others not, placing polished metal disks into narrow slots near the central display. Visions of Vegas and slot machines danced into his head. "I thought we would be alone. No one said anything about all these people here. It only takes one to sound the alarm."

"If I had, would you have come?"

He thought it over a moment. "Hard to say, but I see your point."

"Now you know why that particular detail was kept from you."

Carter choked down his fears and did his best not to attract attention to himself. "Fine. What is it we need to do to shut the power systems down?"

Zoar-Wrel pointed at a free terminal. "There's one over there. It shouldn't take long accessing the central mainframe program database. Once you do, you won't have much time."

He stopped in mid-stride. "What do you mean I won't have much time?"

"The moment you access the primary transmission systems," she replied in an emotionless tone, "receptor grids will start to analyze your DNA signature. In short order, they will figure out if you're not a member of the Overlord species, or an approved humanoid mainframe control tech."

A burst of anger flared in Carter. It was all he could do to keep from screaming at the top of his lungs. "That's more than a little important. When were you going to tell me, when they line us up before a firing squad?"

"Don't get emotional. Our present task is what matters."

"This is getting worse and worse." He marched over to the unoccupied terminal. His proximity to the electronic device activated it. Carter looked at the display, then back at the Overlord. "Why can't you do this?"

"I already said. DNA. Mine would be picked up in a second. Central Command knows I'm not authorized in this area."

Feeling the weight of the moment, Carter turned back and studied the screen.

"Here," Zoar-Wrel said. She handed him a metallic disk about the size of a silver dollar.

"What's this?"

"Too long to explain. Slip it in to the receptor."

When Carter did as he was told, the screen, blue at first, went dark for several seconds before a list appeared. Categorized alphabetically, he scanned through the titles. It took him a moment to realize it was written in English. "That's strange."

"What?"

Though Zoar-Wrel's voice didn't register alarm, Carter thought he picked up on a hint of concern. "The text. I can read it."

"It's part of the disk's programming. I altered it just for you. What you see are the command codes needed to redirect the transmissions dishes. The signals will still be going out, but in a different direction. Once the connection has been broken, that's when the ships and planetary installations throughout the empire will start to shut down."

Carter had to admit, it was a clever idea. Simple, yet devastating in its effect.

"Turn the blinking red knob clockwise. The action will input the new information. You'll know this when the blue button starts flashing. When that happens, press it twice. The disk will then pop out, which means your job is done and we can get out of here before the DNA tracers detect who you are."

"Piece of cake," Carter said. And just like that, the blue button next to the red one started to blink off and on at regular intervals. *This crazy plan just might work*, he thought.

Without any warning multiple alarms exploded in the room. It was a high-low din that rattled Carter down to the bones. "What's going on?" he asked after looking around.

"They know you're here."

CHAPTER 27

A clenched fist struck Menseratis in the jaw. He spun around from the force of the blow and fell onto the ground. A cloud of dust rose above him.

He slowly got back to his feet and spit out a mouth full of blood. "Is that the best you have?"

"Come on," Sulit-Bay said, his arms held in front of him. "Get up."

A defiant smile formed on Menseratis' bruised face. He couldn't remember the last time he had been hit that hard. In a strange way, he felt a wave of respect for his opponent, something he never thought he'd feel toward an Overlord. Clearly, they were not the lazy, self-indulgent sycophants he thought they were. Not only did they appreciate a good fight. They could give one as well.

White hot pain exploded in Menseratis' side when he came again to his feet. He instinctively brought his hand to the spot and held it. The area felt warm and sticky. Blood. He must have landed on something sharp, like a rock jutting out of the ground or something else that sliced his side open.

The Overlord, on the other hand, only bore a trace of the fight. His military tunic had been dirtied in a couple of places, and a slight tear in the seam between the arm and shoulder formed when he rolled out of the way of a blow launched toward his mid-section.

"Give up this fight," Sulit-Bay baited him. "You cannot possibly win against our master race."

Menseratis ignored his taunt and threw another punch at his opponent. Like before, the Overlord easily dove out of the way. The only thing he hit was air, which he paid for with his body. Sulit-Bay swung around with his leg and caught him in the knee. A pop sounded, and Menseratis collapsed onto the ground, writhing in agony.

"Enough," begged Taliah. Menseratis noted her look of horror. "Stop while you still can."

Despite the pain, Menseratis shook it off and struggled once again to his feet. He assumed the same fight position as before.

Wiping off a light sheen of perspiration from his forehead, Sulit-Bay smiled in response. "I had been contemplating how much I would enjoy killing you. I was wrong. Here now, face to face is much more pleasurable. Seeing someone die little by little is like a show that doesn't end. And I hope it never does. The things I will do to your world. A retribution ship is too good for your people."

Menseratis dove for the Overlord. He may have been weakened by his attacks, but he wasn't defeated yet. He threw his arms around Sulit-Bay's torso and knocked him to the ground. The two struggled against each other, one trying to break free, the other doing his best to hold firm. Punches to the side and chest were thrown in both directions, most not having an impact, until Sulit-Bay's struck the spot where Menseratis had been injured. Like before, a flash of pain tore through his body, and he released his adversary.

Sulit-Bay took advantage of the opportunity offered him, and kicked Menseratis in the head. Once again, he found himself on the ground. Another kick hit him square in the mouth, knocking out several teeth. He tried to crawl away from the Overlord, but it only emboldened his opponent. An even stronger kick to his side knocked the air out of his lungs.

Gasping for breath, Menseratis put his head down on the dirt and closed his eyes. As the blows came at him again and again, a strange thing happened. He could almost see his prostrate body on the ground from above, like he had somehow detached from himself. Not far away, Taliah watched in horror as the fighter she had respected from the arena matches had been systematically brought down one hit at a time. How much longer, he wondered, would she let this go on? She had the weapon, and could use it against the Overlord whenever she wished. He hoped with every fiber of his being she wouldn't.

"Enough!" Taliah shouted as she choked back her anger. "One shot and he's dead. Isn't that what you want?"

"No!" Menseratis rebuffed her. "I finish this my way." He waved her back, and she reluctantly obeyed.

Refocusing his body's energy inward, the pain in Menseratis' body faded. The gash in his side mended itself, and three new teeth emerged from his bloodied gums. A warm sensation flushed through every organ, every muscle and tendon, until the injuries he had sustained from the conflict healed. In his mind, he played through the style and forms of attacks used against him, and in a millisecond, developed counter-measures he could use against the Overlord.

"Get up," Sulit-Bay goaded him once again. He bent close

just to make sure Menseratis heard him. "Yes, let's finish this thing. All of it. You, your people, the insurrection."

Without a word, Menseratis rolled over and moved into a crouching position. He tilted his head to one side and studied his confident opponent. "Yes, let's finish this."

He came at Sulit-Bay like a gore ox at full gallop. The Overlord, surprised by his unexpected aggressiveness, back peddled away from him. It didn't help. Menseratis' balled hands struck the Overlord's face again and again. When Sulit-Bay attempted to strike back in return, Menseratis easily avoided the blow that had previously inflicted maximum damage.

The arena fighter spun around and struck the Overlord in the back. Stunned a moment, he coughed up blood.

"That is your proximal digiterus organ. You are now bleeding internally."

Sulit-Bay held his side, obviously in tremendous pain. "I don't understand. I had you. Every punch I threw landed on a vital spot. You couldn't have lasted much longer. Now..."

"You forget, Sulit-Bay. My species has the ability to regenerate. That is the reason I reached the final arena match."

Like a projection shown at an accelerated rate, Menseratis landed one blow after another against the Overlord. In the head, in the stomach, in his chest, no place was safe. Sulit-Bay attempted to repulse the rapid-fire attacks, but his efforts were futile at best. He merely deflected one, only to get hit ten more times.

Bones broken, organs smashed into jelly, the Overlord finally fell onto the ground too weak to move. His filter gills wheezed as he attempted to breathe, but they were so bruised and swollen, only a fraction of the air he needed entered his circulatory system.

"How does it feel?" Menseratis asked as he stood over him. "To live in the shadow of death as others watch."

Sulit-Bay let out a laugh racked by pain. "You cannot win. We have controlled the destiny of a thousand worlds for seven generations. My death will not stop that."

"You are right. It won't. But Carter Stone's life will."

"At the end, you speak in riddles? Carter Stone is dead. You killed him. How can he stop the Raxion Union?"

"One word." Menseratis bent close. "Resurrection."

Confused by what he meant at first, Sulit-Bay's eyes widened. "No. It's not possible. The implants."

"Have been removed. As we speak, he's in the Positron Center, shutting down every power system in the Raxion Union."

"Nooo!" Sulit-Bay cried out.

This was the moment Menseratis had waited for since his abduction and forced combat in the arena. The moment when the victor had turned into the defeated. He raised his steeled hand, and struck the Overlord's windpipe, crushing it in an instant. Sulit-Bay gasped for breath in a desperate effort to stay alive, until his faraway gaze fixed on the distance.

He was dead.

Menseratis stood up in triumph. He looked over at Taliah, and said in a soft voice, "Final match, mine."

* * *

"Finish inputting the data," Zoar-Wrel said in a dispassionate tone. Carter wondered how she could remain so cool under the blare of high-pitched sirens and flashing lights. "It will take them a few minutes to triangulate your precise location."

Carter didn't have to be asked twice. He pressed down on the blue button both times. When the disk popped out, he slipped it into his pocket, then followed Zoar-Wrel in a hasty retreat towards the exit.

Fortunately for him, it only took a moment for his eyes to adjust to the darkened corridor. Unfortunately for him, the same creature as before was still there, blocking his way.

"What should we do?" Carter asked.

Zoar-Wrel pulled out a strange-looking device from her pocket. "My instruments tell me additional guards are moving in this direction. Our best chance of escape is if you grab his weapon and shoot."

"Is that the best you can suggest? The only result I see is that it will get me killed."

"Nevertheless, you don't have any other choice."

The alarms continued blaring in Carter's ears. There was no time to lose. He drew in a deep breath and then tiptoed his way toward the guard. What looked like a weapon lay nestled in a holster at his side. The problem was that one of his hands rested on it, ready to be pulled out at a moment's notice. Then an idea popped into Carter's head. He reached up as far as he could and tapped the guard on his version of a shoulder.

Startled, the creature spun around. Carter dropped down low and grabbed the holstered weapon. When the guard realized what had happened, it was too late. He stared down the business end of his own sidearm.

"How do I use this thing?" Carter asked.

"The same way you use your weapons on Earth," Zoar-Wrel

snapped back. "Just pull the trigger."

Carter's finger found the curved piece of metal and pulled it hard. A sudden flash of light filled the corridor. A second later, the guard lay on the ground, dead or unconscious. He didn't care which, so long as the behemoth had been eliminated.

Shouting sounded in the distance, growing louder, until Carter heard security personnel demanding if anyone had spotted an intruder. Carter's short-lived feelings of triumph evaporated. They needed to get out of there, and fast.

Peering around the corner, three guards came straight for them.

"There they are," one of them yelled.

Both Carter and Zoar-Wrel fired several shots, then ran in the opposite direction down the colonnade. The enemy's response was more than predictable. High intensity clusters of light flew past, detonating all around them.

"Hurry," Zoar-Wrel shouted.

Carter did his best to keep up, but she was by far the faster runner.

A concentration of blasts inched their way closer toward Carter, until the concussion wave knocked him to the ground. "Zoar-Wrel," he shouted after her.

As though she could see from behind, the Overlord stopped and turned around. She did her best to keep the enemy fighters at bay, but that proved difficult. With the advantage of numbers on their side, they easily ducked behind a stone column, while another of their group fired back. When she darted out of the way, they moved again toward their position.

"I can't hold them off forever," Zoar-Wrel complained.

Still stunned by the blast, Carter tried to shake off its effects.

Clarity didn't come quickly.

"Come on. Get up."

Suddenly, several other guards appeared at the opposite end of the corridor.

When they pulled out their guns, Carter dropped down and fired a couple of feeble shots at them.

Several plasma bursts flew past Carter's head, missing him by inches. "You'd better think of something quick. We can't last out here much longer." Then a horrible thought popped into Carter's head. Now that the job was done, nothing was stopping Zoar-Wrel from leaving him behind.

Carter took aim and shot at a shadowy target in the distance. The guard dodged the blasts and fired back in return. If he didn't figure out something soon, he would remain on the Arena Planet for a very long time.

"I don't understand it," he said to the Overlord. "I shifted the dishes, but there's still power in this place. Maybe they didn't really move."

"They did," Zoar-Wrel replied after she avoided a couple of close hits. "Power transfers are in transit. It takes time before the energy in them is used up."

"I hope so."

In the blink of an eye, the lights above went black. Then another, and another. As the colonnade went dark, the shooting stopped.

CHAPTER 28

In the sudden darkness, Carter stood alone with Zoar-Wrel. A high window panel filtered a hazy light down into the colonnade. Carter watched as the Overlord security forces shook the now impotent weapons in their hands. Carter pulled the trigger on his pistol. Nothing happened.

"It's finished!" said Zoar-Wrel, her filter fins humming. "The resistance movement will attack now. The Overlords ships are now as helpless as Nins on a Dobnob tree."

"You can't get more helpless than that," said Carter, noting the excitement on his companion's face. "Come on. Let's get out of here."

Carter and Zoar-Wrel found their way outside the Positron Center. Some of the resistance fighters had landed their crafts while others hovered overhead, ready to fire at any uncooperative Overlords being rounded up and forced to sit on the ground.

It wasn't until this sight that Carter truly felt the surge of joy run through him. They had won. The Overlords were helpless now without their energy source.

A pair of resistance pilots who'd landed their crafts ran over to Carter and Zoar-Wrel with their weapons raised. "Hands in the air!" one shouted.

"I am Zoar-Wrel, the mother, and this is Carter Stone, the one who brought down the energy source."

The two resistance pilots stared for a moment, then dropped to a knee and preformed some type of salute, placing three fingers on their right shoulder.

Amongst the Overlords, Carter saw a familiar face. Ywen-On waved at them quickly from where she had been forced to sit on the ground with her hands on her head. Beside her, he saw Han smiling in his direction.

"That Overlord there and the human," said Carter to the two resistance fighters. "They are with us."

Ywen-On and Han stood from where they sat and quickly rushed over to them.

"We've done it!" Ywen-On said. "The empire our people built is crumbling."

Han reached out and shook Carter's hand. "You are a hero, my friend."

The two resistance pilots stood, celebratory grins on their faces. One of them spoke. "You'll be happy to hear that the Overlord fleet is adrift and helpless. Every ship our resistance fighters find can do nothing but surrender. Without weapons and shields and their main energy drives, they have no choice. Even a single fighter ship can bring in an entire Overlord command vessel.

Carter's joy ebbed despite all the good news and excitement around him. Taliah was still unaccounted for. The last time he'd seen her, he had sent her off with Menseratis to hide. But what had come of that? Had they hidden away successfully?

"I must leave you all for the moment," said Carter. "I have to find Taliah."

Ywen-On nodded. "I detect a strange bond between the two of you."

Carter looked over his shoulder as he headed off. "Your detectors are well tuned, Ywen-On."

"Thank you," she said, accepting the compliment.

"Remember," shouted Han. "Love for a person must extend to the crows on their roof. And my friend, persons from other worlds may have very strange crows."

Carter spun and gave his Chinese friend an appreciative nod. Before he could worry about Taliah's alien customs, he first had to find her. Make sure she was safe. Then he could discover if her heart beat for him as his did for her.

* * *

Taliah spotted Carter coming towards her and Menseratis' position. She'd seen the rebel fighters overhead blasting the Overlord's ships from the sky; she knew that Carter had done it! He had shut down the energy source. Today, the Raxion Empire was breathing its last.

"Menseratis, would you mind carrying me a ways, as if I'm injured."

The warrior from the Kohlani system gave her a strange look. "Whatever for?"

Her eyes turned back to Carter. She heard him call out her name as he continued to search, unaware of her eyes on him.

"Are you as perceptive in matters of love as you are in warfare, Menseratis?"

She glanced at him. His bewildered look turned into one of amusement.

"Now, carry me" said Taliah with a wry smile. "Please..."

In Menseratis' arms she lay limply, eyes closed, waiting in anticipation.

"Over here," shouted Menseratis.

Moments later, she heard the crunch of Carter's feet against the jungle floor.

"What's happened to her?!" came Carter's panicked voice.

"She single-handedly brought down three Overlord trackers, but a fighter craft shot a concussion weapon very near to her. I'm afraid she was struck full force."

Very nice, she thought. *Carter's wounded warrior girl from Axinar IV.*

Taliah felt her body transferred gently into Carter's arms.

"I'll go for medical help," said Menseratis. "I'm afraid her injuries are extensive."

"Please hurry," said Carter, desperation filling his voice. She felt her body held tenderly in his arms and heard Menseratis' feet racing away. Slowly, he lowered her down onto a grassy patch of ground. His hand came to the side of her face and gently stroked her cheek.

"Taliah, please hold on. I promised you I wouldn't die, and here I am. The Empire is fallen. Both our worlds are free now. And... the two of us."

It took all her strength to keep the signs of the happiness she felt inside from showing on her face.

"I want to tell you something, Taliah. If you can hear me, know this—I love you. You asked me to do a hard thing. To die and trust your words that I would be brought back to life. Now I'm asking you... don't die on me. You may not feel the same about me as I do for you, but I at least want to say thank you.

Thank you for believing in me. For trusting me enough to play such a crucial role in your plan.

"But if you do feel the same as I feel for you, I want to know about it. You have to tell me. I want to hear your voice."

Taliah opened her eyes. Carter's mouth dropped in surprise. "Taliah?!"

Her arms shot out with all the quickness of her warrior instincts and grabbed him by the back of his head. In one deft motion she pulled his lips into hers as she bolted upright. She kissed him with all the pent up passion of a heart no longer enslaved, no longer under the claws of an oppressor. She was free. Free to live as she pleased with the Raxion Empire crushed under their feet. And with this newfound freedom, she wanted what any normal being wanted, no matter what world they were from: to be in the arms of those who mattered most.

She knocked him onto the ground, her lips still pressed against his. Finally, she forced herself to pull back. Just long enough to say words she needed to say.

"On my world, when two people are in love, one moves into the home of the other and they are declared bonded for life with a simple promise of commitment toward one another. What are the customs of your world?"

* * *

Carter smiled up at her. "Earth's customs?" He thought a moment. "Boring. Completely boring. Let's stick with yours. But currently, I have no home."

"Can you acquire one? We have the wealth of the fallen Overlords at our fingertips. Surely a home on Earth could be purchased for the two of us. I would very much like to see your planet, *Earth*. And the sooner the better, if you know what I mean."

She bent and kissed him again. This time Carter pushed her gently away to speak.

"You've only known me for a month. Are you sure you're ready to be... bonded to me?"

"On Axinar IV, we bond only when the time is right. I've not bonded with any man because my people needed me to fight. And fighters have hard lives not suited to living out a commitment of love. But on my world, when times of peace arrive, and we know the time is right... we do not hesitate to secure a good mate. Much like a hunter when seeking out its prey. He strikes as quickly as the opportunity arises."

"So I'm your prey?"

A hungry look washed over her face. Carter sensed she was about to attack him with her lips again, but held her at bay with a hand to her shoulder.

Her expression soured. "You don't want me?"

"No, no. It's not that." He looked deep her into eyes. "I know of a place we could live back on Earth. A place where I've always dreamt of building a home."

"Take me there," said Taliah without hesitation. "And please, remove your hand from my shoulder. It's in the way."

Carter lifted his hand, and the warrior girl's lips found their victim once more.

* * *

A cool wind swept through the open cab window as Carter drove his newly purchased black pickup truck down a rutted dirt road in the middle of the Alaskan wilderness. He'd always wanted a pickup truck... and his own dirt road.

"I'll need to patch up our new driveway. A lot of rain and thunderstorms up in these parts."

His bride, Taliah, stared out the window. "I've spotted six hooved beasts that look like they would taste very good cooked over a fire."

"Those were elk. And yes, they're very good eating. But you won't need to cook them over a fire... at least, not the kind I think you're describing. On Earth we have a room in our homes called a kitchen."

"I wasn't speaking of cooking them," said Taliah, "I was speaking of you cooking them. On my world, the women do the hunting, and the men do the cooking."

"I see," said Carter. "Perhaps we could... bring our worlds together and both do the hunting and cooking."

Her hand reached out and grabbed his leg. "I'm more than ready to bring our worlds together. Can this land rider go any faster?"

His foot hit the gas, and the truck lurched forward in a burst of acceleration. The last thing he needed now was a blown-out tire.

"This is beautiful land," Taliah observed. "I can see why you chose this place. Bountiful food sources and endless water. The forests are gorgeous."

"It's not as serene as the countryside that surrounds Han's village, but it has its charms."

"Yes, it did possess a certain majesty that reminded me of Axinar IV, but Earth is my home now. She squeezed again on his leg. "I look forward to learning the customs of your world almost as much as I anticipate teaching you mine."

Carter's head spun. Where was the cabin?

It suddenly appeared as they drove into a clearing. Two stories tall, built of solid logs, the large A-frame home stood majestically, back dropped by a tall snow covered mountain in the distance, and miles and miles of untamed forest.

It was everything he'd ever dreamed it to be.

Carter parked the truck at the base of the wood stairs that led to the front entrance. A huge wrap-around porch lined the bottom of the cabin. The place was perfect. A million miles away from New York City, and his old life. Never would his boss know to find him here. This was a place they could both start their lives over again in the serenity of the Alaskan wilderness.

"Stay in the car," he told her.

"Why? Is there danger?"

"No," said Carter. "I have to perform one of our Earth people's customs."

He popped open his door and made his way around to her side of the truck. From his pocket he pulled out the cabin key and held it in his hand. Opening the passenger side door, he lifted her from the leather seat, then carried her up the six steps to the porch.

"I very much like this custom," she said, looking up at him. Her green eyes sparkled with specks of vibrant red. "But you must set me down, for my world has a custom that I must show you."

"I'll set you down, but only once we've crossed the threshold of the door." He slid the key into the lock, and with a twist the door creaked open. He couldn't help but grin as he took in the beautiful A-frame's huge living room, complete with the double-wide fireplace. It was just like in the brochure, only, it was so much larger than the pictures suggested.

He looked down at his wife of several hours... or whatever her people called it on Axinar IV.

"Welcome to our new home," Carter said with a measure of pride in his voice.

"This is a home greater than any princess could ever dream of on my world." Her eyes scanned the living space with awe, before turning back to Carter. "Now, it is my turn to teach you a custom of my people. One that goes back to the dawn of our history."

Taliah, swung her large braid of hair over her shoulder, then looked up at Carter with a fierce fiery gaze. Without any warning, she pulled her tunic shirt over her head then threw it at Carter.

He reached out to grab it, but when he did, she stepped up to him and shoved him back so hard that he fell against the door.

He stared at her, puzzled amusement marking his face. "What is *this* custom?"

Taliah crouched low. Carter wasn't sure if she was going to spring at him, or dart away.

"It's called lovemaking. I think you can figure it out." She grinned. "But first, you must catch me."

She pushed away from him and darted off toward the back of the cabin, flinging her clothes from her like an animal shedding its skin. Her uncovered form disappeared through an open door.

Carter threw the tunic shirt in his hand onto the ground. He'd managed to survive the Arena Planet, he was pretty sure he could manage this new challenge.

Ready or not, he was going to find out.

ABOUT THE AUTHORS

Mike Lynch's first book, *Dublin*, came out in 2007, followed by *When the Sky Fell* and *American Midnight*, and *After the Sky Fell*, published by Silver Leaf Books. He has also written several other novels, including *The Crystal Portal*, *After the Cross*, and *Love's Second Chance*, as well as an assortment of novellas, short stories, and writing articles in various publications. Mike currently lives in the San Francisco Bay Area with his wife and two children.

Brandon Barr lives in Southern California with his wife and three sons. He is the co-author of three books with Mike Lynch, including the first book of the Sky Chronicles, *When the Sky Fell*. Brandon's short fiction has appeared in Ray Gun Revival, Residential Aliens, Digital Dragon Magazine, and other venues. When not writing, he's often found listening to his sons' fantastical stories of trolls, dragons, and starships. He suspects there may be a future Hugo or Nebula award winner amidst his young protégés, Stay tuned.

CPSIA information can be obtained at www.ICGtesting.com
Printed in the USA
BVOW08s0914070816

457915BV00002B/5/P